NEW DIRECTIONS 42

New Directions in Prose and Poetry 42

Edited by J. Laughlin

with Peter Glassgold and Frederick R. Martin

 A New Directions Book

ACKNOWLEDGMENTS
Grateful acknowledgment is made to the editors and publishers of magazines in which some of the selections in this volume first appeared: for Russell Haley, *Islands 25* (Auckland, New Zealand); for Isabella Wai, *Cumberlands* (Copyright © 1979 by the Pikeville College Press); for Donald Westlake, *Seaweeds and Constructions Anthology Hawaii* (© 1979, Seaweeds and Constructions, Honolulu, Hawaii).

James McManus's prose poems "Antonio Salazar Is Dead" (Copyright © 1979 by J. L. McManus) originally appeared in a larger collection of the same title published by Syncline Press (Chicago).

"Thirteen Drawings from the Norman Holmes Pearson Collection" appear by the kind permission of The Beinecke Rare Book and Manuscript Library, Yale University, and Aleksis Rannit.

"Twelve Poems" by Sylvia Townsend Warner (© 1979, Susanna Pinney and William Maxwell) were brought out by Chatto and Windus, Ltd. (London) in 1979.

Manufactured in the United States of America
First published clothbound (ISBN: 0-8112-0783-8) and as New Directions Paperbook 510 (ISBN: 0-8112-0784-6) in 1981
Published simultaneously in Canada by George J. McLeod, Ltd., Toronto

New Directions Books are published for James Laughlin
by New Directions Publishing Corporation,
80 Eighth Avenue, New York 10011

CONTENTS

MODERN POETRY IS PROSE
(BUT IT IS SAYING PLENTY)

Third Populist Manifesto

LAWRENCE FERLINGHETTI

I
Most modern poetry is prose
as is this poem
and I am thumbing through a great anthology
of contemporary poetry
and 'The Voice That Is Great Within Us'
sounds within us mostly
in a prose voice
in the typography of poetry
which is not to say it is prosaic
which is not to say it has no depths
which is not to say it is dead or dying
or not lovely or not beautiful
or not well written or not witty
It is very much alive
very well written beautifully written
lovely lively prose
prose that stands without crutches
of punctuation
prose whose syntax is so clear
it can be written all over the page

in open forms and open fields
and still be very clear
very dear prose
in the typography of poetry
(the poetic and the prosaic intellect
masquerading in each other's clothes)
Most modern poetry is prose because
it walks across the page
like an old man in a city park
And walking through our prose buildings
in the year three thousand and one
one may look back and wonder
at this strange age
that made poetry walk in prose rhythms
and called it poetry
Most modern poetry is prose because
it has no *duende*
no soul of dark song
no passion musick
Like modern sculpture
it loves the concrete
Like minimal art
it minimizes emotion
in favor of understated irony
and implied intensity—
And how often does poetry today
rise above the mean sea level
of the darkling plain
where educated armies
march by day?
Ezra Pound once decanted his opinion
that only in times of decadence
does poetry separate itself from music
and this is the way the world ends
not with a song but a whimper

II
Eighty or ninety years ago
when all the machines began to hum
almost (as it seemed) in unison
Whitman was still singing
the song of himself
the song of our self
even as the speech of man
began to approach
the absolute staccato of machines
and the hard rock and punk rock
of electronic existence
Whitman was a holdover
(though even Emerson said the 'Leaves of Grass'
was a mix of the 'Bhagavad Gita'
and the *New York Herald*)
And Sandburg was a holdover
singing his poems
And Vachel Lindsay was a holdover
drumming his chants
And Wallace Stevens was a holdover
with his harmonious 'fictive music'
And Langston Hughes was a holdover
And Allen Ginsberg a holdover
chanting his mantras
singing Blake
And Kerouac a holdover
with his 'Mexico City Blues'
which could indeed be sung
as a drunk sings
And there are others everywhere
jazz poets and jism poets
poetic strummers and wailers
in the streets of the world
making poetry of the urgent insurgent Now
of the immediate instant self
the incarnate carnal self
(as D. H. Lawrence called it)
But the speech of most was caught up

in the linotype's hot slug
and now in the so cold type of IBM
(movable type that doesn't move)
while we continue longing for the nightingale
among the pines of Resphigi
I had not known prose
had done-in so many
Lost in the city waste lands of T. S. Eliot
in the prose masturbations of J. Alfred Prufrock
in the 'Four Quartets' that can't be played
on any instrument
and yet is the most beautiful prose of our age
Lost in the prose wastes of Ezra Pound's 'Cantos'
where aren't *canti*
because they can't be sung by anyone
Lost in the pangolin prose of a Marianne Moore
(who called her writing poetry
for lack of anything better to call it)
Lost in the great prose blank verse
of Karl Shapiro's 'Essay on Rime'
and in the inner city speech
of William Carlos Williams
in the flat-out speech of his 'Paterson'
and in the Ivy League elitisms of Robert Lowell
with his weary Lord Weary
and in all the poetry critics and crickets
of *The New York Review of Books*
and of *Poetry* (Chicago)
and every other poetry review
none of whom will commit the original sin
of saying some poet's poetry is prose
in the typography of poetry
just as the poet's friends will never say it
just as the poet's editors will never say it
the dumbest conspiracy of silence
in the history of letters

III
And in that 'turning inward'
away from the discredited clichés
of 1930s politics
Freud and Jung replaced Marx
as intellectual deities
among poets and painters
their radical aspiration turned inward
to the 'discovery of the unknown'
within themselves
and the poets turning inward to record
their personal 'graphs of consciousness'
Robert Creeley and Charles Olson began it
the prose-poetry of introspection
and a whole school followed it
and in the beginning was Ginsberg
who almost singlehandedly
took poetry in a new direction
picking up on Whitman's mimetic
'casual spontaneous utterance'
And the San Francisco poets continued it
and the New York poets continued it
and the objectivists continued it
and the projectivists continued it
and the constructivists continued it
and everyone continues it
in the high academies
and in a thousand little reviews
and big anthologies
spoonfed by the National Endowment of the Arts—
And that poetry which recorded
the movement of the mind
became the norm of American poetry
(the mind somehow assumed to be basically poetic)
and it was a wonder in the mouths
of such as Allen Ginsberg
in whose packrat omniverous mind
was the seismograph of genius
and if the mind be comely

all that it utters is comely
and divinely sings
in moments of ekstasis
But the graph of more pedestrian poets
could only be walking prose
and the boat of love breaks up
on the shores of everyday life
And the Collective Unconscious
remains uncollected
though poetry has many great voices
many modes and many voices
the best of whom cite music
as their ideal
but few do sound the deep refrains
and leitmotifs
of our still mysterious existence—
too many of our best brains
simply not equal to
the mass confusion of our colliding cultures
nor to the confusion
in how to tell poetry from prose
(that most persistent question running through
the literary meditations of this century)
except as William Carlos Williams saw a way
(in reading Marianne Moore)
of getting around this question
by ignoring it
(He too disliked 'poetry')
and so turned his back on it
in favor of the spoken verse
of the great American idiom

IV
Most modern poetry is prose
but it is saying plenty
about our 'soul-less civilization'
and what it has done to our free men
to our Eros man and Eros woman
the anarchist in each of us
who is the poet in each of us—
Most modern poetry is prose
but it is saying plenty
about how the soul has gone out
of our cities
out of our buildings
out of our streets
no song among the typists
no song in our concrete architecture
our concrete music
(And Mumford was right of course—
architecture reflects the soul
of civilizations—
But man reflects it
more than buildings
as women reflect it—
the true temples of flesh)
Modern poetry is prose
but it is saying plenty
by its very form and tone
about the death the self dies every day
the poet in each of us
that's killed a little every day
'You killed him you sonofabitch
in your Brooks Brothers suit!'
So wailed Kenneth Rexroth long ago
with poetry-and-jazz in San Francisco
And so wailed the young Allen Ginsberg
in his 'Howl':
'What sphinx of cement and aluminum bashed open
        their skulls and ate up their brains and
        imagination?

Moloch! Solitude! Filth! Ugliness! Ashcans and
    unobtainable dollars! Children screaming under
    the stairways! Boys sobbing in armies! Old
    men weeping in the parks!'
And so wails today a still wild voice
inside of us
a still insurgent voice
lost among machines and insane nationalisms
still longing to break out
still longing for the distant nightingale
that stops and begins again
stops
and begins again
stops
and resumes again

It is the bird singing that makes us happy

THIRTY-EIGHT INDIANS

Or, The Penalty for Treachery

WALTER HOWERTON

Execution of the Thirty-Eight Indians at Mankato Following
the Suppression of the Sioux Uprising

> *"William J. Duly of Lake Shetek es-*
> *caped after a desperate encounter."*

Coming east, Mr. D—— entered Chicago through the back door.
Climbing the back stairs, he unbuttoned his pants and gripped
himself with his trembling right hand. He worked his lever up and
down, back and forth, side to side. The sound of his feet on the
stairs made his fingers grasp and his palm sweat to shove the lever
all the way. He reached the platform at the top of the stairs and
anticipated the doorknob with a firm downward thrust on his own
handle. His balls hurt like childbirth. He was already twelve hours
overdue.

"Dakota?" He whispered into the keyhole. "Dakota, where were
you? Last night?"

"Out on the prairie. On my back."

"Doing what?"

"Looking at the stars."

"I was here."

"I wasn't."

"I know." He fingered the keyhole. "Can I?"

"No. Wait."

"Now?"

"Almost."

"Now?"

"Just. Yes."

"Is it unlocked?"

"Yes."

Mr. D—— tripped the latch, shoved the door, leaped into the room, sprang onto the bed, sucked his mouth into her, came, recoiled, and spit. Thick globs of other men clung to his moustache. "Dakota?" His stomach heaved and Mr. D—— slipped to his knees at the foot of her huge bed, but he did not vomit. "Dakota?"

She rolled off the bed, stood, spread her feet far apart, oozing little white spheres which snail-tracked her thighs.

"Thirty-eight Indians," Dakota said. "Thirty-eight Indians."

Something grabbed Mr. D——, and he did vomit. The dark hand from under the bed lost its grip under the warm, slippery contents of Mr. D——'s stomach. He looked down and saw the blade of a knife disappear under the fringed edge of the chenille spread. Mr. D—— screamed. There were heavy chuckles from under the bed.

"Dakota," he said. "Dakota, you're all I have. I'm old, and my family died young. I'm tired." Mr. D—— got up and buttoned his pants as he ran. "Dakota?" he shouted back.

"Thirty-eight Indians," Dakota said. She smiled, and it was a fine unreconstituted smile.

The chuckling Indians rolled out from under the bed, cash in hand. They paid her and ran after him.

1

"after a desperate encounter in which
he killed Lean Bear."

"At least a white man could stuff it down the leg of his pants," Lean Bear muttered as he rolled out of his blankets alone. His wife was sick; she had been sick for many days and now was in the tipi of her mother. She couldn't dance for him last night, and she could do nothing for him this morning. And he always woke with an erection when there was the smell of paint in the air. Yet, he couldn't bring himself to do anything about it. "Perhaps she will die," he said. "And maybe it will help if I piss." Squaring his breechclout, hunching to hide his lump, he hurried out. "Just one day. Give me just one day, Running Wolf," he wished. "Call it off for just one day, and I will ride in and swap something for pants. Or I will see the missionary. He would give them to me and be happy. And we could start this tomorrow." The water he made steamed. He walked back to camp, back to his empty tipi, hunching a little less. He got his paint pots and sat down. It helped to dip his fingers into the paint.

Lean Bear had drawn one of the isolated farms near Lake Shetek and would go alone. That was fine with him; there would be no jokes along the way. "What you leaning on these days, Lean Bear?" "Leaning on your fist these days, Lean Bear?" "What was Lean Bear doing out by the horses last night? Leaning up against his favorite mare!" "Get food. Get horses. Get rifles if you can, and don't forget ammunition," Running Wolf had said. "I want some of those pants," Lean Bear whispered to his horse. He heard the heavy blows of an ax off to his right and veered away.

The ax is as simple and rigid as a Puritan. It has two parts: a head and a handle. The head, actually a metal wedge sharpened to a blade at the tapered end, is called a bit. A well-sharpened bit is said to have a good edge on it. A clean bit with a good edge will do more work than a dull and rusty one. The ax handle is hard wood. It is rubbed smooth and oiled. The bit of an ax can be as sharp as the edge of a flaying knife or a straight razor, but if the handle sheds splinters or raises blisters, the ax is useless. It requires two hands to swing an ax—one to anchor it and the other to aim the blow. A rifle requires two hands for the same reason. But a man with two hands and an ax has a better chance of surviving the wilderness than a man with two hands and a rifle. A man with an ax can clear a space for himself, build a fire, make a shelter, a trap, or defend himself; a man with a rifle knows the frustrations of power. The puritanical ax keeps the hands busy and the brow sweaty.

"Well kept, it is as reliable as the Commandments," Mr. D——— told his son. He honed the bit against the whirling stone. "And farming takes space. Trees stand on space." Then he walked down the path alone and disappeared into the trees. "Good. Good. Good." He grunted with each swing.

Hache is the French word for ax. Its diminutive is *hachette*, or, in English, hatchet. A hatchet is a small, short-handled ax. Like most diminutives and derivatives, the hatchet is impure, tainted. Railsplitter Lincoln used an ax; Washington did it with his little hatchet. A hatchet is little more than a symbolic tool. When peace is made, a hatchet is buried; an ax isn't wasted. For the settlers it was a trinket from the first. The land was gained with handfuls of hatchets and beads; it was possessed with an ax. They knew a hatchet was useless in the face of the wilderness. It is a trick of the devil. It is gripped with only one hand, and who knows what the other hand might be doing?

Lean Bear dismounted out of sight of the house. He took the hatchet from his belt with his right hand. It was an old hatchet and had been traded from white to Indian, Indian to Indian, Indian to Lean Bear. The old owner had called it *The Mayflower*. The name meant nothing to Lean Bear, but he kept it.

His breechclout bulged again. He urinated behind a spruce tree, but it didn't help. Even though he had other things to do, he fell to his knees. He had just begun to run his hand up and down.

"There's a red Indian over there on his knees playing with his little thingee."

"Over where?"

"Right behind that tree."

"You liar."

"I'm not."

"Show me."

Lean Bear knocked them both in the head. It helped to hit them with the hatchet. He was swift; there was no noise; he was that swift. There was still the sound of the ax away in the woods.

Lean Bear ran toward the house, ducked the narrow window, and flattened against the wall. Inside he heard the rustle and hum of a woman alone. He tucked *The Mayflower* into his belt and stepped in front of the open door, rubbing his stomach with his left hand and pointing to his mouth with his right. He was careful to stay outside, polite. When she heard him, she turned to look. Her mouth opened, but she did not scream. She motioned him inside. Lean Bear nodded and kept rubbing and pointing until he had squatted near the fire.

She was as swelled and white as what they called bread. She talked to him in her language. "Words that aren't understood are best left in the quiet place where they come from," he quoted the Old Fathers to her. But she didn't understand; she shrugged and kept talking. The Old Fathers had also told him that words are the arrows of frightened or angry women and that a blank face is a warrior's only shield in this war with women. Lean Bear let his eyes roam the room. He saw the Sunday trousers hanging on the wall and smiled.

Her back was to him; she stirred the pot on the fire. He moved swiftly and silently, shedding his breechclout as he went. When she turned and saw him she did scream. Blankly, Lean Bear sunk *The Mayflower* into her face. He steadied her head with his left hand and worked the blade free of the bone.

Mr. D——— used up his ax against the trees.

The Sunday trousers were like the whites; they looked simple enough from the distance. But Lean Bear couldn't figure them out. He stuck his legs into them. But, then, what should have been at the waist was around his feet. He pulled his legs out. He held the trousers up in front of him. He fiddled with the waistband and fingered the suspenders. He tried them again. *The Mayflower* was in his way, and he put it down. He considered a prayer but there was no time to make a prayerstick. He looked at the woman. Escaping the Sunday trousers, he walked over to her. He grabbed her by the ankles and dragged her into the middle of the room. He pulled up her skirt and squatted beside her. He rubbed the hair on her legs. He rubbed her drawers, then he pulled at them, carefully sliding them down to her knees, then up again, then down to her ankles and back to her knees, and finally back to her waist. When he thought he knew how they worked he pulled them off of her completely, then put them back on. He was sweating. He pulled them off of her again and sitting with his legs parallel to hers pulled them over his own feet and up to his waist. He repeated the process with the Sunday trousers. But he couldn't figure out the suspenders. When he stood, the trousers dropped to his ankles. There was a noise. He turned. He tried to step out of the Sunday trousers as he backed away. Lean Bear stumbled over the woman's awful, white, hairy legs.

"Good. Good. Good," Mr. D—— said, swinging the dulled ax.

There were other incidents that day. There are monuments to prove it.

"One negro, Godfrey, who lived among the Sioux"

Going north, Godfrey, once he had escaped, got to the Ohio River. And when he got there he was ready for it, once the sun came up and he took his readings, because his Daddy had had a vision.

"Now, I have seen a vision. I say the Lord God has give me a sign."

"Aaa-men. Aaa-men."

"I say THE Lord God has spoke to ME."

"Yes. Yes."

"And what He hath SIGnified"

"Oh!"

"What He hath sigNIfied"

"Lord, yes."

"That what He hath signiFIED"

"Oh, yes."

"Is"

"Is?"

"IS"

"What? What? What?"

"Is that there is two things every nigger got to know. Two little things. Two little secrets. Just two and only two little things. Simple things. And do you know what they is? Do you know?"

"No. Tell it. Tell IT!"

"You sure? You sure you want to know the secret? The secret that was handed down to me up there on top of that mountain?"

"Mama, there ain't no mountains round here. Not one. He's up there lyin bald face bout visions and"

"And if I was you, Godfrey, I would shut up that mouth. If God don't whomp you, you're Daddy's gonna when he gets done."

"Yessum."

"Do YOU want to know the secret?"

"Tell it. Right now, yes."

"Well, if you sure, here tis. The Lord God come to me in the form of a cotton boll. I was settin there and all twonce this here cotton boll—this very one—was touched by Him and every filament lit up and"

"Aaa-men."

"and the voice of the Lord God come roarin outen the depths of that cotton boll like thunder and the earth stood stark still. BOOM! The Lord say. BOOM! BOOMBOOM!"

"Oh. Oh. Praise the Lord."

"And the Lord say, 'I have a vision for thee and here tis. Thee and thine, all thine kind, must heed this message. Every fiel' nigger. Every house nigger. All thee niggers listen up and I, thy Lord, shall hand you down the secret of freedom and of heaven. For there is two things thou's gotta know would all yuns get to the glory place and set down with me.' And then He say in a voice of mystery, 'The Jerdan River runs east to west.' And I tell you, brothers and sisters, I couldn't make a thing outen it. Then, He put in the important thing. 'Heaven on the north side of that river. Get that? I'm only gonna speak it once.' And I say, 'Yes, Sir,' and He went on. 'Thee and thine all gotta get from the south side of that river to the north side to get home. You know which way north is, brother?' And then I got hold of what He meant by it. Every nigger here is gotta learn what way north is. So, He say, 'That river runs east to west just like the course of the sun. When you get to it, you wait for the daylight. When the sun comes up, face that water. The sun gonna be on thy right hand, just like my onliest son, the Lord Jesus, is on mine. When the sun be's on that right and the ruver runs to thy left, you know you's facin north.' Yes, lord. YES, Lord. Yes, LORD."

"Yes, Lord. Yes. Yes. Aaa-men."

"But I said there's two parts to the secret. And that's only the first part of it. So, THEN, the Lord say, 'Angels got wings to fly over that water. And because my onliest son, the Lord Jesus, walked over that water and he's white, the white folks got feets to walk it. But you niggers, you gotta swim it. You know how to swim the water?' And I understood that part too. Then, the Lord touched me with the power of swimmin and handed me the task of teachin you all. And I say, 'Thank you, Lord. Thank you.' "

"Thank you, Lord. Thank you!"

"So, there's just two things we gotta know. We gotta navigate, and we gotta swim. Two little things."

Godfrey learned north and how to swim to it with the others. His Daddy baptized them all with a swim across Little Cotton Mouth Creek, which was known after that as Niggers' Little Jerdan.

Godfrey swam north into Ohio. He had thought about New York and Detroit, but he had heard there was trouble there over jobs the whites wanted. He didn't want any of that. He knew he wasn't a field nigger anymore, but since he wasn't a nigger, he couldn't decide what he wanted to be. So, he shied west and ended up among the Sioux. The Old Fathers had told them a tale of a black man who healed the Indians long before the whites came. And the Sioux thought Godfrey had a finish like a high silk hat. They let him stay. They laughed at his stories. They liked for him to tell the one about how the whites all thought that they wanted white women above all. They would laugh and laugh and shake their heads at that one.

After the raids, Godfrey ran away. He slept the night by a river. The next morning, the sun rose on his left. There was no way he could cross it, and he was captured. Over the next few weeks those who weren't killed or captured surrendered.

"After the surrender of Camp Release a commission was appointed by Gen. H. H. Sibley, who had command of the forces on the Minnesota frontier, for the trial of the Indians implicated in the massacre.

"This commission tried 425 Indians and half-breeds on the charge of murderous participation in the

> massacre, and of these 321 were con-
> victed, 303 being sentenced to death,
> while the remainder were sentenced
> to pay lighter penalties. The East set
> up a cry that these people were pris-
> oners of war, and that it would be a
> crime against the nation to permit of
> this wholesale execution. As a result
> an investigation was made by the
> general government out of which
> grew an order from President Lin-
> coln."

"What in the hell are those people trying to do out there, any-
way? Don't they know there's a war on? Don't they know we have
all we can do back here? Haven't they heard of Fort Sumter?
They're going to mess around with their damned Indian problems
till they mess us right out of the Union. Indians! What are those
people going to do when I start sending the freed niggers out there?
Cause that's what I'm going to have to do. There's too much bad
blood here for me to set them loose in the East. They'll have to go
west. Even Jefferson knew that. There's too much against it here,
and it seems to me that there's room-a-plenty out there for every-
body. That's the way the story goes, and I believe the story. Don't
you? What part of it are they in again? North or south?"

"North, sir. Minnesota, sir. West of Illinois, sir, and a little
north."

"I know where Minnesota is. It just slipped my mind is all. There
are so many places out there. I mean it's big out there. That's what
we're fighting for here. To keep it all in a piece. And those people,
the people in Minnesota, you know what they wanted to do?"

"What, sir?"

"They wanted to kill off something better than three hundred of
the savages. Three hundred and three to be exact. Can you imagine
that? And they want to call THEM savages. Well, I won't have it!
My own boys are out there dying like flies, getting gunned down
like so many passenger pigeons, and they want to worry me with
hanging three hundred Indians. I tried to be reasonable about it. I
said, 'Let's hang Jeff Davis. Then we can worry about hanging In-

dians.' But no. So, damn them. Just damn them all. I told them they could hang thirty-nine. I figured it out on the basis of a humane percentage. I tried to be fair to everybody. Half of the braying jackasses in the East were raising hell anyway, and I had to do something. There's a war on, a war for the Union. Besides, I've got to go on being the president just to pay that woman's bills. Anyway, I told them to hang thirty-nine. But I've decided, and I'm not going to let them do that much. I'm in charge here. I have to be in charge. I'll show them I'm in charge. Let them hang thirty-eight Indians. I'm the president; I'll pardon one of them."

"There's a nigger in the bunch, sir. You want to pardon him? That would sure be one way of letting people know what your line of thinking is. You want me to send through a pardon for the nigger?"

"And why should the nigger get special treatment? What I'm aiming at is to get the niggers treated pretty much like everybody else, wherever I put them. Democratic. We're fighting to save the Union, and the Union is democracy. No sir. You treat the nigger just like the rest. Put all of the names in my hat, and let Todd come in here and pull one out. That's fair. Don't you think?"

"Yessir. Sir?"

"What is it?"

"Do you think the boy's arm is long enough to reach the bottom of the hat?"

"You think this is a joke?"

"No sir."

"Then get out! Get out!"

"Yessir, sir."

> *"After thirty-nine of the most guilty*
> *had been selected, one was pardoned*
> *by President Lincoln."*

> *"William J. Duly of Lake Shetek es-*
> *caped."*

Mr. D——— shoved the crate from Dakota's piano across the back door and ran down the alley, looping his suspenders over his shoulders as he ran. It was Sunday; the trains would be infrequent, but he ran toward the platform. There was a crowd. The children carried pennants and tiny baseball bats or wore plastic helmets.

"What day is it?" Mr. D—— asked.

"Opening day," one of the children said.

"Old fool," a voice behind him said, and there were heavy chuckles.

When the train came, Mr. D—— hesitated, then jammed himself into an already packed car. None of them could get on behind him. The train lunged at the city's middle. Mr. D—— smiled; he was lost in the crowd and headed for vague buildings.

"Mommy, that man's little thingee is sticking out."

Mr. D—— buttoned his fly. He would call Dakota from The Loop.

> *"Not an Indian was self-convicted. All swore positively to childlike innocence, and affected amazement that they had been accused. One negro, Godfrey, who lived among the Sioux, was among those. His plea of innocence availed him nothing, as he, like Cut Nose, was known to have committed some of the most monstrous crimes ever charged up to the account of a fiend."*

"You laughed," Godfrey said. "When I told you, you laughed."

They all laughed. Of course, they remembered what Godfrey had said, but they remembered the words of the Old Fathers, too.

> "Laugh and the world laughs with you.
> Cry and you cry alone."

2

"Dakota?" Mr. D—— whispered when she answered.

"What?"

"Again?"

"No. Not now."

"Why?"

"I have to go sing. I've been asked to sing. They even sent me a cute little jacket to wear. I have to do it. They need me. Can you call me back?"

"But Dakota. Who? I need you. You're all I have. I've told you. I"

"Later, I said. Later."

"Can you just talk? Just talk for a minute?"

"But the train. The train. For a minute. The train."

He unbuttoned. She talked. Someone banged on the side of the booth. He looked up. They were all there, all thirty-eight, in a line, and each one was waving a Roosevelt dime.

> "Passing from crime to punishment
> the scenes that followed the sentence
> were without parallel in our national
> history."

The laughing Indians were all put into a single cell.

"That was something," Cut Nose said. "When they told about Lean Bear and that white lady's drawers, that was something. Can you imagine it? Can you figure out why he even did a thing like that? Maybe he'd been drinking. I don't know. With his wife sick and all, maybe it was just too much for him. But the real thing was the way that man enjoyed telling about it. I have noticed that they love to tell about things like that. 'My ax was dull from the morning's work, and it took four stout blows to sever the savage's head.' That's what Godfrey told me he was saying. And when he got to the part about Lean Bear having those drawers on, I couldn't help but laugh."

Several of the others chuckled, too. They drew long pipes from leather cases.

"But we had a reason for doing what we did," one of the others said. "Lean Bear went too far. What reason did he have? It was against the will of Running Wolf what he did. Running Wolf is our chief. His word is law. Yet, Lean Bear wasn't left to suffer here with us. He escaped through the hole the ax made, and he left us here. It is a mystery," he concluded.

"We must ask him," a third Indian said. "It is a mystery, and we will ask him the answer. We, too, will escape soon. Is that not what they said? That we will all go together?"

The others nodded and smiled.

"Fire," Cut Nose shouted to the guard. "Pipe fire." A pan of coals was passed into the cell.

> *"They were treated with humane consideration by the officials in whose charge they were, pending the final act."*

"I feel sorry for the whole damned lot of em," the younger guard said. "Don't get me wrong. I ain't sorry because they're gonna die. But they don't know what's happenin to them. They don't know they're gonna die. It's like a game for em. Listen to em in there, laughin and talking. I swear I don't understand em. Do you?"

"Ain't hard for me," the other guard said, "but, then, I'm older than you. They're savages. That's what makes us different from em. They don't know the diffrence btween life and death. They're ignorant. They know what's bout to happen. They just don't care."

"Well, if that's the truth, I'd like to know their secret."

"I told you. They're ignorant. And another thing. They goddam stink, and I would rather be off fightin Johnny-goddam-Reb than here with a bunch of stinkin Indians. Least then I'd be up against somethin human, somethin that's afraid to die. Somethin that don't stink unless it's dead."

"They still puzzle me," the younger guard said.

"Don't puzzle me none. But then I'm older. They're savages," the older guard said and went off to walk his tour.

> *"The condemned received much comfort from the Christian influences thus brought about them."*

"General Sibleysir, I am here seeking your assistance in the furthering of the work of the Lord." The man put two boxes on the desk. "And I have come to you because I know you have here the wretched savages who are about to meet the Maker. I would like to have the opportunity to put those poor beasts into contact with the redeeming suffering of Our Lord before the fateful day arrives and the trap is sprung. Would that be possible? I feel that it is my Christian duty to continue this work among the savages, a job of work· begun by the very Pilgrim forefathers on the lip of the continent more than two hundred years ago. What do you say, sir?" The man waited, smiling.

"What exactly is your proposal, sir?"

"Well, General Sibleysir, through my extensive travels in the missionary fields carrying the word of the Lord to the heathen hoards of Asia, I have come across a miracle which I hope to put to use to animate the sufferings of Our Lord for the eyes of the nonbelievers. Let me show you." He removed the lid from one of the boxes. "I have here a box full of holy figures of Our Lord in the posture of crucifixion. You will notice that they are not rigid and, in fact, that they are as limp as our own pitiful flesh. That is because they are made of gum rubber, the miracle substance from Asia, which can be melted and poured into a mold, producing any shape one would like. In this case, the suffering Christ. Here. Hold one of them. You will see what I mean."

"You mean to give one of these to each of the savages?"

"In a manner of speaking, yes. But that is not all there is to it." He opened the other box. "Here I have the crosses themselves. These were crafted by a group of the wretchedly enslaved in the Port of Charleston. Each cross is hand shaped from native American pine. First-rate craftsmen, the poor enslaved blacks. I have seen extraordinary examples of their work during my travels in the missionary fields of Africa. In one village, for example, I saw an extraordinary pagan figure so intricately carved that all of the parts were movable and reversable so as to give the figure a variety of roles and attitudes in various of their ungodly ceremonies. Once when I saw it, it was a man. Another time, it was very obviously a woman. Did they cut off the genitals in a fit of mad passion? I asked the question very nervously, I can tell you. And the laughing natives—and their ignorant laughter is that of the most innocent of children—showed me the trick. When the figure was in its female attitude, one had but to run his middle finger up inside those parts to release a catch which made the genitals fall away. The very canal into which the finger was inserted was the inside of the shaft of a penis which could then be fitted neatly between the legs of the figure. When the figure was male, one had but to grip the penis and twist and it would fall away. Poor, clever, and devil-directed souls. They had quite a laugh at my expense, I can tell you. But when I designed this holy project, the blacks were the first to come to my mind because of their obvious abilities. And they fashioned these crosses as well as I knew they could, including the placement of this wire along the length of the cross. That is where your Indians can be of use in the good work. What better way to use the natives of this or any other place than in the work of Our Lord?"

"What will they have to do?" the general asked, bending the Christ double between his fingers, thumping its lolling head and fingering the soft thorns across its brow.

"I know that they can do no more than simple tasks. They will simply insert the wire the length of the figure, thus, attaching it to the cross. Then they will add these small brass tacks to the hands, and the job will be complete. Here I have a completed sample. You will notice that the wire forms a crank at the foot of the cross. Turn it. Yes. There."

"Like this?"

"Just like that. See how the figure writhes when you turn the wire? What better way is there than this to depict the suffering of Our Lord to the ignorant savages of the world? And what better way than to have some from among them construct it? It is, after a manner of speaking, a way for them to help themselves. Don't you see?"

"I see," the general said, spinning the wire left and right. "I see."

"And General Sibleysir?"

"And, yes. I think I can arrange it. But you will have to excuse me just now. My captain has some problem with the—the arrangements—and I must see him now."

"Thank you, General Sibleysir."

"Yes. Tell him to come in as you go out, would you?"

"We have, General Sibley," the captain said, "a problem concerning the disposal of the Indians."

"Lincoln?"

"No sir. Nothing like that. In fact, I think the government is now on safe philosophical and humanitarian grounds, especially since the total number has been reduced. No sir, this is a mathematical problem. On the one hand, we have the pleasant matter of subtraction in that we will be reducing the total number of living savages by thirty-eight. The problem arises out of the proper way to dispose of thirty-eight Indians. It is a problem of symmetry. The gallows we have designed and constructed is square. That is, it has four sides. Four into thirty-eight will not go. Four into thirty-six, yes; into forty, yes again; but not into thirty-eight. You see the problem?"

"Yes, and . . ."

"And it leaves us in an esthetically weak position. Off balance is, perhaps, a better way to put it. It is my opinion, sir, that we all have to do our parts to preserve a sense of order in the current chaos, the war in the East and so forth. Do you see what I mean? There will no doubt be photographers and illustrators here. And, since our purpose is to use the event as effectively as possible . . ."

"What do you propose?"

"That is why I came to you, sir."

"Obviously, Captain, I have faith in your discretion."

"Yes, sir."

"So, what do you propose?"

"Well, obviously, sir, two legs of the square will contain ten savages and two legs will contain nine. My question is, would it be preferable to have the tens and nines adjoining or parallel?"

"Parallel ranks seem better fit to a military occasion, Captain, don't you think?"

"The same, sir, but I wanted to be sure our thoughts coincided on this matter. Thank you, sir."

"I'll make a note of your concern on the record, Captain."

"Thank you, sir."

> *"The condemned in the main accepted their fate philosophically."*

Godfrey snapped the long stem of his pipe and threw off his blanket. He took off his headband and moccasins, his breechclout and leggings. He scrubbed his face until the paint was gone. Naked, he walked to the barred door.

"Hey, you. Soldier-sir!"

"What is it?"

"Look at me."

"Crazy goddam Indians. Come over here, Wes, and lookit. One of em's took off all his clothes."

"I ain't," Godfrey said.

"What you mean, you ain't? If it ain't somethin crazy to shuck all your goddam clothes in December I don't know what is. Ain't that right, Wes?"

"I mean I ain't no Indian. Look at me, sir. Look. Do I look like a red Indian to you?"

"Man, you are really crazy. You better cover your self up. You gonna get cold and die."

"But look at me. I ain't no Indian. Do I look like one of em? I mean, I'm a nigger. I'm a slave. I ain't no Indian. You ever hear of the Fugitive Slave Act? Did you?"

"Hear him, Wes? Crazy as a damn loon."

"But look at me! Look!"

"Indians," the guard said, and walked away laughing.

Cut Nose wrapped a blanket around Godfrey's shoulders and led him away from the door. "You are like a child," he said. "There is a song taught to us by the Old Fathers. It is a song for children. You came to us in the body of a man; so, we treated you like a man and you never heard it. But the Old Fathers have given it to us, and it is a wise song. Of course, it is a song the women sing, but those are often the wisest of all songs, even though it is men who gave them the songs in the first place. Warriors sing the songs of yesterday and tomorrow; but the women have the voice of the life we live, and they give that voice to the songs. It is the songs left to the women by the Old Fathers which allow us to live the days as we find ourselves in them. They are the mother songs. And when men are away from women, when there are no women, men must sometimes be each other's mothers. So, I will sing it to you." Cut Nose sat, forcing Godfrey to sit with him. He took Godfrey's blanket away and clutched the naked man to his chest, rocking him. The sounds began high then became low, even, comforting.

> "Would you like to swing on a star
> Carry moonbeams home in a jar
> And be better off than you are
> Or . . ."

All of the others smiled to remember.

"This is not our way," said the first Indian in the line. He took a rubber Jesus from one box and a pine cross from the other box and handed them to the second Indian.

"No," said the second Indian in line. "Our way is definitely better." He fastened the rubber left hand to the cross with a tack and passed the cross to the third Indian.

"I agree," said the third in line. "If we did it our way, I would do more than put this tack in the right hand. I would put in your tack as well. Then, I would insert the wire." He handed the flapping Jesus to the fourth Indian.

The fourth in line poked the wire through the soles of the feet. He pressed the rubber legs against the foot of the cross with his left thumb and pushed the wire with his right hand. He forced the wire up through the soft legs and body, guiding its progress with his left thumb. At first, he had hurried the wire through the soft legs and body, and the wire had emerged through some of the rubber shoulders and chests. Now, he took particular care to see that it came out through the top of the head, where it was supposed to.

"You are holding up the line," the third Indian said.

"But I have the hardest job," said the fourth. "Besides, it is not our way to hurry."

"But we aren't doing this our way. I told you that," said the first.

"Yes, but look at it this way," said the fourth Indian, fastening the wire under the staple at the top of the cross, "I am doing what I can to preserve our way, even here." He passed the completed crucifixion to the fifth Indian.

"I can understand what you are doing, what you are trying to do," said the fifth in line, "but my part puzzles me. I attach this card to it with a piece of string, but the card does nothing. It is a waste," he said, knotting the string around the rubber knees. "If we were doing this our way, we would waste nothing." He passed it on.

"I agree," said the sixth in line. He put the Writhing Jesus into a box with others.

There were six lines, each line with six Indians. When a box was filled, Godfrey took it and added it to the stack beside the barred door. Cut Nose brought an empty box and set it beside the sixth Indian in line.

"If only we could do it our way," said the first Indian.

"If we could at least sit in a circle," said the second in line, "we could laugh or sing."

"I agree that it's easier to laugh in a circle than in this line," said the third in line, "but you are holding up the line."

> "As the day for the executions drew
> near the condemned were permitted
> to receive friends."

Face-like-a-Hawk had been chosen. They sat around him in two circles of nineteen.

"You know we must escape," Cut Nose told him. "And we have chosen you to help us. The whites have chosen the way in which we must die. We must dance without the ground beneath our feet and that is not a bad way. But in killing our bodies, they would kill our spirits also, trapping them inside us with their loops of rope. That must not happen. And if we are to escape, you must help."

Face-like-a-Hawk agreed.

They smoked a pipe with him and asked that he bring certain necessary things: paint for their faces, the feathers of eagles, bear grease for their hair.

Mr. D— boarded the El in the Loop with the northbound crowd. Pennant wavers packed comfortably around him. Standing on his tiptoes, he looked back through the train. They were there, smiling, in the next car back, their thirty-eight left hands looped through the overhead straps. They, too, had gotten pennants and waved them at him when they saw him looking. The pennants carried the name of the opposing team.

3
"Let Duly do it."

"But he's not official."

"They're only Indians. Let him do it."

"But sir . . ."

"No. It's an order, Captain. I order you to appoint Mr. Duly the honor. It might help him, and it will sure as hell help us. We won't have any special duty pay to hand out. We do need all of the money we can get for the war back east. Let him do it."

"Yes, sir."

> *"and for the fatal scene upon the scaffold arranged their hair and painted their faces with painstaking effort."*

The cell was thirty-eight Indians long, one kneeling behind the other. Godfrey was at the rear, since his hair would not need braiding.

"Do you think there will be whites there?" the nineteenth Indian asked.

"To watch? Of course. Which of them would miss it?" the twentieth Indian replied.

"No," the nineteenth Indian said. "I mean, do you think there will be whites where we are going when we leave here?"

"I'm sure not," the twentieth Indian said. "They are too strange for that place."

"There is so much of that place that it would drive them crazy trying to get hold of it all," the thirtieth Indian said, and they all laughed.

They went on braiding slowly and carefully and were quiet for a while.

"One thing troubles me still," the nineteenth Indian said.

"What's that?" asked the eighteenth.

"Do you think the People will become farmers like the whites?" the nineteenth asked. "After we are gone?"

"If they do, I am glad that I will never see them again. Farming is a terrible thing to do to the land," said the second Indian. "It opens great spaces between the people and the trees. Then the spaces have to be alternately attacked and coaxed like an unwilling wife. It is a strange thing, the way they do it, and a terrible thing to do to the land."

"I agree," said the thirty-fifth Indian. "But do you think it is farming that makes the whites crazy?"

"Yes," said the thirty-sixth, "definitely. It disturbs their thoughts. Take the case of us. Why else would they do what they have done to us? We are agreeable people. When we saw how many of them there were, we moved to the place by the river where they told us to go. We did not hunt because they said that they would supply us with all that we needed. And they didn't. And when they didn't keep the bargain and we asked them why, they laughed just like children. When we went out to collect the things we needed, they said we had done a bad thing. Certainly people got killed, but they have to be crazy to think that it is a worse thing to eat than to be hungry. Yes, farming makes them crazy."

They braided feathers and ribbons into each other's hair.

"But, then, perhaps they have always been crazy," the fifth Indian said. "Look at their fires. An Indian builds a fire just big enough to do what needs to be done. An Indian builds a fire that a man can stand astride to dry his leggings. But the whites! They build fires you can't stand near. It would crack the leather in your leggings." They all laughed. "Yes, I think they have always been crazy," the fifth Indian said, and they all agreed but one.

"That would be too easy, just to say that they are crazy," the sixth Indian said. "I think, perhaps, that has been our mistake. Because they are different, we think they are crazy."

"You are a very wise Indian and should live a long life," said the tenth Indian.

"Tell them that," laughed the sixth, and they all laughed with him.

> "The condemned were never too
> deeply distressed to enjoy their
> pipes."

"It is the pleasures of this life that one must know how to enjoy," Cut Nose said, packing his pipe full of pungent willow bark. All of them were sitting or reclining on the ground beside the gallows. "They are all watchers. Look at them." The others nodded, smiling around their pipestems.

> *"Thousands of people witnessed the execution."*

There was an artist who sketched the scene. And the Suffering Jesus sold well, each with the details of its manufacture on a small white card which was tied to the knees of the rubber Christ. It was the twenty-sixth day of December, 1862, at Mankato, Minnesota.

> *"At the appointed moment the con-*
> *demned arose from a sitting or reclin-*
> *ing posture and walked with a steady*
> *step to the death trap, apparently*
> *glad the suspense was to be ended."*

Mr. D____ shifted from foot to foot, flexing the fingers of his right hand. He counted their seventy-six feet as they climbed from step to step to the platform.

Cut Nose made the sign of luck and courage to Godfrey before they bound his arms.

The gallows were square. Ten of the Indians were placed along the north beam, ten along the south. Nine went to the east beam and nine to the west. After they had been arranged and bound, they began their death song.

> *"William J. Duly of Lake Shetek,*
> *whose family had been murdered by*
> *the savages and from whom he es-*
> *caped after a desperate encounter in*
> *which he killed Lean Bear, was priv-*
> *ileged to spring the trap that sent the*
> *thirty-eight murderers into eternity at*
> *one stroke."*

Mr. Herman of St. Paul drew it in pen and ink and sold the drawing to *Harper's Weekly*.

"The bodies were cut down after death was pronounced and carried to a sand bar in the Minnesota River, where they were buried in one trench."

When he had uncovered them all, Face-like-a-Hawk cut the nooses from around their necks; then, he ran away.

"Some brave Indian," Cut Nose said.

"We must catch him and thank him," the thirty-sixth Indian said.

"He knows we thank him," said the fourteenth.

"Yes," said Cut Nose, "but I think we should find the other one, the Wasichu with the sweaty hand. He helped us, too."

"Yes," they all agreed, and they left the river running toward Mankato. Godfrey, of course, was the last to escape the trench. He had to catch up with them.

They entered Mr. D——'s room shortly before dawn. He began to run.

> *"Thousands of people Mr. William J.*
> *Duly. Thousands of people."*

Mr. D——— got off the El at Addison Street with the crowd. He walked with them, hemmed in, herded, comfortable.

"Where are we going?" he asked.

"You aksin me that?" said the boy.

"Yes. No. I suppose. Can you tell me?"

"We're goin to the ball game, man."

"Where's that?"

"It's where it is, man. Where do they play the ballgame at?"

"That's what I asked you. Where are we going?"

"That's what I thought you aksed me. Where else do they play the ballgame but at the park."

"What's the park?"

"Man, you gotta be kiddin. Where you at?"

"Chicago?"

"That's it, man. And in Chicago they play the real ballgame at Wrigley Field."

"Wrigley Field."

"That's it, man. That's where we're goin. If you ain't drunk, man, you one dumb hunk of dude." The boy laughed.

They had passed through the gate. After talking to the boy, Mr. D——— was no longer comfortable. There were chuckling sounds everywhere. He stood on tiptoes. He couldn't see them anywhere. But he could hear. He panicked. He turned left, right, ran down a flight of stairs, down and around, until he was alone in a long tunnel. There was daylight ahead and he saw the thirty-fifth, thirty-sixth, thirty-seventh Indians and Godfrey go up into it. He ran after them. "Thirty-eight Indians," he said. "Thirty-eight Indians and thousands of people. Ha." As he approached the doorway, he could hear the hum of the crowd. His hand began to sweat. "Ha!"

But the Indians had taken the field before he got to the end of the tunnel. There were ten on the first base line; ten between second and third; nine from first to second; nine more from third to home. Around them, the thousands rippled up and away, seeking their seats.

Mr. D——— jerked a thirty-eight-ounce Louisville Slugger with a concave barrel and stickum on the handle from the batrack by the dugout steps. He stepped onto the field and advanced to the plate. There were a few scattered cheers.

"And now, ladies and gentlemen, as selected by special team ballot, Miss Dakota Morefield will sing our national anthem nthem them."

The Indians had tiny Louisville Sluggers; they raised them in thirty-eight clenched right fists. At the plate, Mr. D—— whispered her name, then came to attention, propping the knob on the bat handle comfortably into his crotch and placing his hand over his heart. The crowd rose to its feet, seatcreaks and shuffling. Dakota stood on the pitcher's mound in her satin team jacket. She gripped the microphone with both hands and closed her eyes.

"Oooooooooooooooooooh saaaaaaaaaaaaaa-aaay can you seeeeeeeee-eee-eeee"

The Indians couldn't understand the words and began to stomp; the bells at their knees jingled.

"By the dawn's early liiiiiiiiii-ight"

She forgot the words in the middle, but that had happened to other people. She hummed it and let the bells cover for her.

"eeeeeeeeeeeeeee," Dakota sang. "And the ho-ome of theee braaaaaaa-ave."

She finished. The Indians smiled and began to move around the bases. The thousands resumed their seats. The applause was polite.

"Thank you," Dakota said, moistening her lips with her tongue. "Whew," she said. "That's work." She removed her jacket. The dark stain of her night on the prairie was on her back. That was all. She held the microphone in her fists. "Oh, thank you," she said and took the rounded end of the microphone between her just-moistened lips. The sound system was old; the shock knocked her flat on her back in the grass behind the mound.

The Indians moved toward the mound. "Dakota!" Mr. D—— screamed. He brought the big bat to his shoulder. The Indians continued their inevitable advance to the slow rhythm of the bells, bells, bells, bells, bells. Mr. D—— ran to her and a cheer went up from the crowd.

"Batter up," the umpire shouted.

Mr. D—— looked to the plate. A batter advanced, his helmet sitting squarely on his shoulders, his white drawers bulging. The crowd cheered.

"Unh," said Dakota. Mr. D＿＿ dropped his bat and grabbed the leather sphere that rolled from between her legs.

"Oh," said Dakota. "Oh. Oh. Oh."

"Lawd, Miss Dakota," Godfrey wailed as he danced in from shortstop, "I don't know nothin bout birthin no baseballs." He danced back into position. The balls kept rolling. "Unh," Dakota said. "Unh. Unh. Unh." Mr. D＿＿ gathered them and clutched them to his chest.

"Play ball," the umpire said, and Mr. D＿＿ fired to the plate.

"By God, there are thirty-nine Indians out there," the president roared from his box. "I said thirty-eight. Thirty-eight! No wonder things are in a mess. Nobody listens. I had a plan. I had a dream. I had." His aide quieted him with a whisper and a blow to the head.

"Strike one," the umpire said.

The Indians did their dance. They did their tableau of Babe Ruth pointing away from home; they did Jackie Robinson coming into the majors. They did Lou Gehrig's farewell speech in Sioux dialect. They squared and crouched, ready for every pitch. They began to sing. Not one of the thousands could understand one word of it, yet, they cheered. They clapped. They laughed till they cried.

"I'm home team," Mr. D＿＿ cried. "Home team always gets last bat. First to field, last to bat. That's me. I get last bat." He fired to the plate. He delivered another pitch. He stood in the middle of the square of Indians and delivered and delivered and delivered.

"Strike one," the umpire said.

"It's going to be a long afternoon noon   oon," the announcer said.

The Indians waved their tiny souvenir bats and with every swing bells jingled, jangled, jingled. In deep, brave voices they continued their song. It was another song of the Old Fathers.

> "Buy me some peanuts and crackerjacks.
> I don't care if I never come back!"
>   come back!"

ome back!"

>   mmme back!"

    back!"

"After a term of imprisonment, the convicted savages who had escaped the hangman's noose, were placed upon a reservation assigned to their people beyond the borders of Minnesota."

AIRBORN

OCTAVIO PAZ AND CHARLES TOMLINSON

In the spring of 1969 four friends—Charles Tomlinson, Jacques Roubaud, Edoardo Sanguineti, and I—met in Paris, for the space of a week, in order to write the first Western renga. Renga is the traditional Japanese name for a poem composed by several poets, three or four, who write successively stanzas of three and of two lines, without rhyme, but with a fixed syllabic measure. Our own renga was written by four poets in four tongues and the stanzaic pattern we followed was that of the sonnet, unrhymed and in free verse. After this experiment, Charles Tomlinson and I decided to explore yet another way of approach. We had the idea of writing two series of poems, each one around a theme. The chosen form was once more the sonnet, stricter than that of our renga, but still without rhyme. The real innovation consisted in writing the sonnets by correspondence. Renga in slow motion.

The themes we settled on were House and Day. Then, an exchange of letters: Charles wrote the first quatrain of House and sent it to me, I wrote the second, sent it to him and so on, until four sonnets were completed. We followed the same procedure with Day, which I began. The last sonnet of House was written entirely by me and the last of Day by Tomlinson: each of us brought to its end the series begun by the other.

In the first quatrain of House, Charles alludes, as a matter of course, to his cottage in Gloucestershire, a simple country structure of the eighteenth century which he, with his own hands, has set to rights. I replied, likewise as a matter of course, with a quatrain which alludes to the house of my childhood in Mixcoac, now destroyed, like the rest of the village, by the expansion of Mexico City. Two themes which arose spontaneously interweaved: the house set to rights and the one destroyed. Two kinds of poet, he who lives in a cottage in the country, though this is the civilized English countryside, and he who lives in an apartment in town, though this town is the urban jungle which makes up Mexico City.

It was my turn to begin Day, and I began it with an evocation of a spring day in Cambridge. Charles replied in perfect accord. Then, this English day changed to night, night was succeeded by dawn, and dawn by a Mexican noonday fifteen years ago in whose light Charles and Brenda walked along la calle de Venustiano Carranza and discovered, among the traffic and the people, a source of quiet. Truces and mercies of time in that well of pure water within the poetic memory.

At the same time as we were composing our poems we went on to translate them. The second line of the first quatrain of Tomlinson's gave me a lot of trouble. The quatrain begins thus: "One builds a house of what is there/(horsehair bounded the plaster when horses were)." I understood this to mean that the Tomlinson's house had been the stables of an old manor in the vicinity—famous as having lodged one of the loves of Charles II—and that, during the work of reconstruction, Tomlinson had come across horsehair stuck in the plaster. Consequently I translated: *crines en la argamasa de la caballerizia* (horsehair in the mortar of the stables). Charles undeceived me: no, in the pre-industrial era they used to bond mortar with horsehair. As I'd promised myself not to exceed the fourteen syllables, this elliptical line occurred to me: *con crin ligaban la argamasa—había caballos* (they bonded the mortar with mane—there were horses).

Once our little book was completed we looked around for a title. Brenda Tomlinson suggested *Airborn* (*"Hijos de Aire"*) to us. An exact title: our booklet was an offspring of air. Charles pointed out that the expression contained other meanings: airborne, every poem is made of air (Pound: "I made it out of a mouthful of air"), and an air is a song. But there's even more to it: the day I received Tomlinson's letter suggesting this title, I read a loa of Sor Juana in which Aeolus, god of air, appears:

> I who am presiding god
> of the rarity of air,

whose office is the government
of the Birds' imperium where
through transparencies of space
in wandering varieties,
animated rainbows, they,
little vanities on wing,
people and adorn its sway . . .

Airways are the most used today, as much by travelers as by post. Nevertheless, they have been and are also the traditional ways of poetry: across the thoroughfares of the air, "wandering varieties," the stanzas of the poem are propagated, "animated rainbows." Since its origin poetry has been the art of joining together the echoes of words: chains of air, impalpable but unbreakable. I will add that poetry is further, and above all, an art of breath, inspiration and expiration.

OCTAVIO PAZ

These collaborative poems were the result of a meeting, early one summer in Gloucestershire, when, out of the many words we had thought and spoken, we chose "house" and "day" as the words for a future postal meditation in sonnet form. "House" arose because the stone cottage in which Octavio Paz and his wife were our guests was a place we all felt affection for, and also because at that time the Pazes had no settled house of their own. "Day" was our last day together, when the sky took on a Constable-like activity, the breeze moving clouds swiftly through the blue and involving the landscape in a rapid succession of changes. I think time was at the back of all our minds, and that "day" (time passing) thus came into a natural relationship with "house" (time measured by place). We drove to the station through the green countryside, only to find that the train no longer ran. In the hour or so we had to wait we stole time from time and conceived our little work.

CHARLES TOMLINSON

NOTE. The italicized portions are those written in Spanish by Octavio Paz and translated by Charles Tomlinson. The couplet of Góngora is from E. M. Wilson's translation of the *Soledades*.

HOUSE

> *O hermitage well found*
> *Whatever hour it be . . . !*
> —Luis de Góngora

I

One builds a house of what is there
(horsehair bonded the plaster when horses were)
and of what one brings (the rhyme concealed):
space into its time, time to its space.

Yet we are born in houses we did not make.
(The rhyme returns, a bridge between the lines.)
The sun revolves its buried images
to restore to mind that ruined house once more

time and not I unmade—the rhyme revealed
only by the unheard pace of time,
and fragile yet dissonant against its space.

Time unmakes and builds the house again:
and rhyme, a sun brought, echo by echo, to birth,
illuminates, unspaces it back to time.

II

House that memory makes out of itself
between the spaces of blank time—more thought
than lived and yet more said than thought,
house that lasts as long as its own sound takes:

house, you began in milk, in warmth, in eating:
words must re-tongue your first solidities
and thought keep fresh your fragrance of bread baking
or drown in the stagnation of its memories:

house in which two pasts conjoin and two
hands inscribe their separate histories,
a murmur in search of meaning builds you

where, in a hive of words, time's honeying
flavours and fills with momentary savour
this mouth and mind, this citadel of cells.

III
A self awakened in the press of things:
hacked into elm-bark there I left behind
initials, date: and the marks remain:
they fix a childhood and a war in Spain:

it was the blade of that same war graved deep—
not on the trunk of an imagined elm—
but in my head the red map of the ranges
of its fallen debris and its broken word.

So that to taste again my hope's true fragrance,
leaven of that miraculous first bread,
to hope, yet hope without extravagance

I traced, not with ideas nor with stones
but air and light, the due shape of my going:
houses are meetings and departures too.

IV
Houses that come and go within my head,
the buried seeds that lie there ripening
under my eyelids, houses turned already
to a handful of anecdotes and photographs;

unsteady structures of reflections
in the water of time hovering suspended
through this wide instant where a pair of eyes
travel distractedly across this page:

moving through them I enter my own self,
I am the lamp inside their empty rooms
and like a soul I kindle and extinguish.

Memory is the mind's own theatre.
Outside: the resurrections of the sun:
myself I plant within myself: this present is my habitation.

DAY

> *Sweet day, so cool, so calm, so bright,*
> *The bridall of the earth and skie.*
> —George Herbert

I
Copious tree each day. This one
(July the fifth) grows hour by hour
invisible: a tree obliterated
to be freighted down with future leaves.

Coming to terms with day—light, water, stone—
our words extend a world of objects
that remains itself: the new leaves
gladden us, but for no motive of their own—

merely to be vegetable exclamations,
onomatopoeias of celebration
of the yearly chemical resurrection,

where evening already stains the finished page
and shadow absorbing shadow, day
is going down in fire, in foliage.

II
Scholiasts of dreams, we are the heirs
of the rediscovery of night—return
to origins of the word, dark syllables
from leaves unseen, from selves unheard.

Day dawns through a promiscuous succession
of waves—vowels and consonants—and breaks
down the dikes of language to explode
endlessly outwards and become no word.

This presence is all absences until
we hear it wash against our panes, our walls
and shadows shape the architecture light must fill.

It dawns: with fingerings impalpable
daybreak sets ajar the lidded eye:
raining, it rains into the space of memory.

III
The city wakens to a din of chains,
at the streetcorners light is torn apart
and blind, uproots within the memory
the trees—the days—their leaves of syllables:

crossing Bolivar and Carranza street
in search of the Fuente de la Rana
and the Turkish clock—postcard civilities—
under a sky of fifteen years ago:

through to-ing, fro-ing, passers-by and cars,
courteous philosopher, the clock strikes the hours
tactfully skeptical, always exact,

true to the count and yet false to the fact
of that well within time—time's truces, time's mercies—
even, at this waste hour, still tasted here.

IV
Days that haunt the poem's single day
are like the air revisiting this house
of vocables that you and I designed:
its windows watch an ocean and a sky

to learn what portion of the other's mind
the jet-trails presage: letters are stones that fly
to settle in a wall of which the line
traces an hour, a where, a place of thought.

What is more palpable, the thing we saw
or the images its recollection brought
into the mind to ask us what we are?

Friendship is more palpable than both,
the day that founded it, and time its confirmation:
we go and stay, knowing in that pulsation
we are the measure of its music flowing.

> *Daughter I was of air, already*
> *I dissolve away in day*
> —Pedro Calderón de la Barca

KIMO'S STORY

ISABELLA WAI

Kimo's young master had been married for two months, and the bride was very beautiful. Whenever she smiled, two tiny dimples appeared. Kimo studied the young bride's dimples closely; they are shallower than those of Miss Fox, he thought. Miss Fox loved Kimo's young master, who, however, preferred to marry a human being.

"Kimo, stop staring at me," the young bride said. "I'm Lotus. Not Miss Fox."

"Yes, it's you. Her dimples are much deeper. But you two look very much alike."

It was full moon. The young master was writing in his study, and Kimo was washing his clothes.

"Kimo, please take this package to my uncle," Lotus said. "Here's some money for you to buy a drink."

"My Lady, but it's dark."

"Are you scared of Miss Fox, Kimo? Don't be silly. She won't harm you. She won't harm anyone. She's a little playful, but she's kindhearted."

"Do you work together with her against me?"

"Of course not. Everyone likes you, Kimo."

"Then why do you always send me to deliver this and that at night? Can't I wait till tomorrow?" Kimo, like a frustrated child, asked.

"My uncle will be leaving town at four tomorrow morning. You may wait till then if you prefer. I don't mind."

"That's even worse. I may as well go now."

Whenever Lotus asked Kimo to do anything, he suspected that Miss Fox might be using her to play a trick on him. If she asked him to get her a bucket of water from the well, he worried that her double would push him down the well; no one would come to save him till he was half drowned. Or a badly mutilated face would jump up from the well and smack him on his face. What he hated most was to go to the hill behind the house to gather firewood, because Miss Fox had disappeared into that forest on his master's wedding night. Kimo suspected the forest was one of her hideouts. But she could be everywhere.

Kimo had been hallucinating for a month. Sometimes he dreamed that Miss Fox was plucking him like a bird, greasing him, and frying him for her dinner. Sometimes she seemed to be walking on the roof, and opening the skylight of Kimo's room. She hurled down diamonds and gold, which changed into rocks and brimstone as they thundered down, rattling every plank of his bed. Kimo cried for help and woke up in a shower of cold sweat, still trembling under the weight of his heavy comforter.

In the young couple's room, there was a piece of marble with Miss Fox's name inscribed on it. It was a tribute to honor her. Kimo dusted it every day and brought flowers from the garden to place in front of it. He knelt before it three times a day before he ate, and each time he banged his head on the floor to show respect for her.

"My Lady, say a prayer for me," Kimo begged.

"It will be all right. Don't worry." She smiled.

Kimo jingled Lotus's tip in his coat pocket and left. He turned the collar up and pulled it high to cover his ears. While he was trembling in his coat, he seemed to hear Miss Fox's laughter in the wind. He turned around, but saw nothing. Every man he passed was a threat to him, and every door was a potential danger. A tavern was across the road. Kimo wetted his lips with his tongue and crossed the road.

"Hi, my friend, haven't seen you for a long time." The tavern owner patted Kimo on his shoulder. "You have been hiding at home after dark like an unmarried young girl. What's the matter?"

Kimo mumbled an answer.

It was warm inside. Noisy. Some were drinking by themselves.

At one corner there were two drunks, one thin and one fat, cursing their wives. The thin one kept biting his finger nails and spitting. The fat one had his shoes off and was rubbing and scratching between his toes. By the front wall were three young men drinking with tavern girls. A girl was singing near the counter and playing her lute. Near the back door was an empty table. Next to it sat a drunk, who was half asleep, his head on the table and his hands outstretched. Occasionally he raised his head and burped and said, "Good wine. Beautiful woman. Nice song. That's life." He burped again and threw his head and his arms back onto the table, scattering the peanuts all over.

Kimo sat down at the table near the drunk's.

"A cup of rose wine, Ah Kau," Kimo said.

"Do you want to have a girl sit with you?"

"No women, please, I'm afraid of them all."

"We have a new addition. She's a beauty."

"She might be Miss Fox in disguise."

"She's definitely not a fox," said the tavern owner. "A real woman." He tapped his chest, winked at Kimo, laughed slyly and said, "I know, my friend."

"I don't want any woman." Kimo was almost shouting. "Women and petty men are a source of trouble. That's what Confucius said."

The tavern owner shook his head and walked away.

The year before Kimo had followed his young master, Hon-sun, to Shanghai to visit the young master's uncle. Hon-sun had been attracted to a girl selling fans and cosmetics in her father's shop. Kimo's master stood every day at the streetcorner waiting for the girl's father to leave so that the girl had to wait on him when he got in. The shopowner usually left every day at nine o'clock for his tea break and stayed out till eleven. Kimo always remembered that if one ate his master's food, one had to share his master's worries. The young master might not know that women and the devil were equally troublesome. The girl was beautiful, with dimpled cheeks and dainty hands. Her name was Lotus. She seemed to be hiding behind something all the time, either the pillow case she was embroidering or a fan she put on the counter for that purpose. Kimo followed his master to the shop and hid behind a pillar that stood near the shop.

"Good morning," the young master greeted the girl.

"Father," the girl pushed aside the curtain over a door and called her father, who might be working somewhere in the living quarters. "You've a customer."

"You don't have to call him. He's gone."

The girl seemed surprised.

"Don't worry. Just name a price, and I will pay it."

The girl moistened her lips and said, "But what do you want to buy?"

"Anything. I mean any fan. A fan. That's what I want."

The girl asked for a price almost twice as much as the fan was worth. The young master frowned but paid her.

The next day, the young master returned to the shop again. Again the girl charged him double. Before he stepped out of her shop, she called him back.

"I've overcharged you." She blushed. "Here's the extra money."

The young master smiled.

Every other day, he came to the shop to buy one item, a fan, or a handkerchief, or some rouge. The girl wrapped it carefully for him and used her tongue to wet the corner of the wrapping paper to seal the package. Afraid of ruining the place touched by her tongue, the young master carefully put all the packages in a chest and never unsealed them or touched them again.

One day the young master received a letter from his parents in Hankow and learned that his grandmother was seriously ill. Before he left Shanghai, he went to the shop to see his beloved girl again. But the door was closed. On the door, there was a notice saying that the owner had returned to his hometown for a visit. Regretfully, the young master left with Kimo and went back to Hankow. His mother wanted him to get married before his grandmother died. But the young master would not hear of it.

"My son." The mother fell onto her knees. "A marriage might brighten the house and drive the demon away from your grandmother." She sobbed.

Hurriedly the young master helped her to stand up again and said, "Mother, I will be cursed by the gods if my own mother kneels before me." And he proceeded to tell her his love for the girl in Shanghai.

"My son, you should have told me earlier. It's easy. I'll ask my brother to talk to her father."

But the young master's uncle could not locate the girl or her father. They never returned. And Hon-sun's grandmother died.

For a change of scene, the young master decided to visit his poet friend living on the other side of Hankow. He took Kimo with him.

One day, without giving a reason, the young master asked Kimo to pack and move to a small house about two miles from his friend's house. It was a two-bedroom house. The young master let Kimo have the front room, the bigger and the better lit. Whenever Kimo stepped into his master's room, he felt as if he walked into a shady cave with winds blowing from all directions. He suspected that it might be the headquarters of ghosts and foxes. His master asked him to stay away from his room, especially at night because he had to work on his poems. There was only one small window in the young master's room. It was facing a low stone fence.

One night, Kimo, drunk, returned home and went straight to bed before he fed the horses. Shortly after midnight, he woke up and went to the stable to feed the horses. He saw light coming out from his master's room, and shadows dancing on the stone fence. Kimo tiptoed near the window and saw his master chasing after a girl. She looked like Lotus, wearing the same clothes she used to wear in her father's shop.

The next day Kimo asked around to see if anyone knew a girl named Lotus. There were only two other houses besides his master's in the neighborhood. In the house to the east lived an old woman with her dog, and in the house to the west lived two brothers without any pets. No one had seen any pretty girls around that area.

"My master," Kimo stammered. "I saw a girl in your room one night. I do not want to pry into your affairs. But I'm your servant and should share your worries."

The young master blushed a little and said, "She's our neighbor."

"You are deceived. There are no pretty girls in this area. She must be a ghost or a fox."

"No, do you still remember Lotus?"

Kimo nodded.

"That's she."

"She might look like Lotus, but she is too pale and less pretty. Her dimples are much too deep."

"But she's not doing me any harm."

"Not yet. She's interested in your soul and is taking it little by little from you." Kimo examined his master's face carefully. "You look possessed. Your cheeks are sallow, and you look sickly. You'll lose your soul to her before you even know what has happened."

The young master was quiet for a while, and then his hands began to tremble. "What am I going to do?" he asked.

"Let me hide under your bed tonight. When she comes, I will rush out and stab her."

Helpless, the young master looked at Kimo. "Whatever you say."

The clock struck twelve. Someone opened the window and stepped in. Kimo, dagger in his hand, rushed out from under the bed and made a dash toward the girl.

"Stop!" the girl commanded.

Kimo felt as if a stone hit him and shattered his body into pieces. Everything stopped. Kimo stood paralyzed, with one foot in the air. His tongue hung stiff in his mouth, and his jaws were suspended ajar. He looked like a wax model of a soldier who was yelling as he was plunging into the battlefield. And his dagger was pointing at his own ribs.

"Hon-sun, I don't mean any harm. All I want is to have some fun with you." She turned around and spoke to Kimo, "Drop the dagger, and bring in the wine."

Kimo tested his arms and legs to see if they moved.

"I want to have a farewell drink with your master."

"Get the wine," the young master said.

The girl remained calm and smiled. "Hon-sun, I was sorry for you. I am sorry for all miserable lovers. So I decided to appear in her shape to comfort you. Don't you find me equally charming?"

The young master was speechless.

Kimo served them wine. All the time, he remained silent. His tongue was hanging useless inside his mouth.

After the drink, the girl stood up and said, "I'm leaving now, but will be back on your wedding night. I just want to see who is prettier, your dream girl or me." She flung open the windows, stepped out, jumped over the low stone fence, and vanished.

The next day, the young master and Kimo packed all their luggage and returned home.

Three months later, there was a rebellion in Shanghai and the people fled to Hankow. One morning when Kimo was sweeping the front porch, a girl lingered around the house, hesitating to knock on the door.

Kimo approached her, and she tried to hide her face behind a handkerchief.

"Young miss, can I help you?" Kimo asked.

A draft lifted the handkerchief from her face. Kimo was taken aback. His voice trembled as he asked, "Miss Fox, is that you?" Then he backed up a few more steps. "No, that can't be you. It's daytime. You are supposed to stay away during the day."

The young master, hearing the commotion, appeared in the scene. He blushed and was speechless. Finally he asked, "Are you Lotus?"

"Yes." She blushed.

The young master and Kimo looked at her dimples carefully, and Kimo said they were Lotus's, shallower than those of Miss Fox.

Lotus told them her adventure once they got inside the house. She and her father were taken by the rioters. They killed her father and burned their house. In the middle of the confusion, a girl appeared and took Lotus's hand and ran. The girl could run faster than a horse. Soon people, noise, horses, and fire were out of sight. Lotus could not remember how many miles she had run. Just before dawn, the girl let go Lotus's hand and pointed at the road in front of her and asked her to take that road till she saw someone sweeping the front porch. The one who loved her lived in that house.

The young master's mother seemed to be very fond of Lotus and entreated her to stay with them. In the meantime, she made preparations for the wedding.

The young master showed Lotus the packages he bought from her. "Perhaps you can use some of this," he said.

Lotus shook her head and said, "There's no cosmetics inside any of the packages. Only red earth."

Kimo laughed, holding his stomach.

The young master tore the packages open. Diamonds and gold rolled out. They resembled those worn by Miss Fox.

A month later, the young couple was married. On their wedding night, Kimo, like a knight, guarded the bridal chamber. Drunk, the young master staggered into the room and closed the door. Kimo tiptoed over and pressed his ear to the door and peeped through the key hole.

"You are stinking drunk," the bride said.

The young master held her face close to his eyes.

"Which of us is prettier? Sister Fox or me?"

"You of course." He burped. "But some careless people may not be able to tell the difference between you two."

They laughed and went to bed.

Another bride, accompanied by the matron, approached. Kimo rubbed his eyes. He had not let one drop of wine touch his tongue that night. What had happened?

"Stop." Kimo ordered the matron to stand still as he rushed forward to stop her from knocking on the door of the bridal chamber.

"What's the matter with you, Kimo?" the matron asked.

"Who is that?" Kimo asked.

"The bride. Who else?"

"The bride went in about half an hour ago."

"You must be drunk."

Kimo tried to lift up the bride's veil to have a look at her face.

"Behave yourself." The matron hit him with her fan. "How dare you? Your master is the one to lift up her veil. He may expel you from his house for assaulting his bride."

"What's happening?" The young master was yelling from within.

"You are a careless person too," a female voice inside the room said. "Kimo," the voice seemed to be speaking directly into Kimo's ears. He looked around but did not see anyone. "I've proved to your master that I am just as pretty as his bride," she continued. "He couldn't tell the difference between Lotus and me." She paused. "Kimo, you tried to murder me once and ended my happy days with your master. I will punish you for that some day." The voice died into the distance and blended with the growling from the hills.

"I'm only doing my duty. A servant who eats his master's food should share his worries." Kimo burped. "Well, I don't mind even if she punishes me as long as she puts on a nice appearance."

"Just pray that she won't change into a corpse or a cobra when you take her to bed." The drunk sitting at the next table winked at Kimo and smiled. Two deep hollows appeared on his cheeks. He burped and fell back onto the table.

THE RED ENVELOPE

BETSY ADAMS

PART I

for Deborah Bradford Richardson

1.
The carriage stops at the gate,
the silver shaft centers the stone.
the blood blister is growing, fine fibrils
tracing tumorous growths along her thigh.
Letters are dropped through the rectangle
in the door. Two white envelopes and one red.
She kneels, picks them up, and as always
opens only the red.

Side by side on the table, they lie.
Three in a row, the red, then carelessly thrown
the two white. Ink smudged on one
of the white; a deep purple pus is rising
beneath the smallest of the fibrils where
her crotch meets her thighs.

The letter opener lies in the deep setting
by the window. Unused. Discarded.
The walnut table coverless, brown hues
reflected from the ceiling.

She lies on the worn vellum-like couch
and sleeps. Her hands lie between
her legs, rest heavily on the point
where her crotch meets her thighs.

2.
Inside the room there is milk on the table,
and beside the glass the purple triangle
of cloth cut from the couch. She sits and holds
the lukewarm glass, beads of sweat between
her eyebrows. The refrigerator door closed.

The yellow cat is seated on the floor, looking up.
Waiting. Several times she turns the pages
in the same place over and over in the book
she is reading. The triangle of cloth is not
used as a napkin, but lies beside the red envelope.
The edges of the envelope are not smoothly opened,
but ripped and impatient. The morning sun
is entering the room, making the yellow cat golden
and mellowed, and he decides to dose.

3.
The coffee has become ready and she moves eagerly,
rises to fill the white porcelain cup with the yellow
iris and the green leaves to the brim. It will not
clatter in the basin of the saucer; and she folds
the worn triangle into a small purple square,
shoves it into the folds of the red envelope.
She touches the red tissue paper with the purple ink
with the large bold writing, and pulls at it
in little tugs, as the cat pulls at the dead mouse
he's brought before breakfast to show her.

Great puffs of vapor are still rising from the pot,
and she leans down to stroke the yellow cat;
her pale yellow gown she wore to bed the night before
brushing against the thighs of the sleeping male.

4.
She opens the back of the grandfather clock and takes
the key which hangs by the long twine her father
had hung there for her, and winds the ceaseless thing.
Of course it must not stop, and the tarnish which lies
inside the case is rubbed down not by her, but
by the one she pays to do it who comes in once a year
for such things. Suddenly the organic outside
to this house reaches her: the damp soil, the dead
purple and yellow iris, the earlier daffodils, the small
long-hidden violets.

She never wears a scarf but leaves the whitewash porch
in the loose gown. Passes out the front, around
the house to the side and then to the back, the red
envelope in her hand. The blister on her thigh
is pulsing, and aches more than usual; and she notices
the grass frog which sits at the side of the bright
plastic dish she threw into the yard the night
before, too lazy to rinse it.

5.
She passes to the toolshed, and retrieves the square
spade, with the broken edge; moves toward the field,
and stops where the mown lawn ends and the deep
grasses start. And begins to dig.
The earth gives way easily, as it has rained
the night before, and she thinks it is because of this
that the smell of the flowers is so strong.
She sees the pale green katydid, a very young one
in the center of the enormous purple field flower.
She has never learned the proper names of the flowers,
but recognizes them each year as they come, in succession
after succession: first the violets, then the iris,
wild ones not planted by her; then the white simple
fringed blossoms, and the yellow and white clovers
along with the purple ground clovers; finally the large
queen anne's lace, and her favorite, the blue cornflower.

6.

She does not dig deeply, but she digs widely
enough for the red envelope to fit flatly into the
square hole in the earth. The purple writing on the face
is placed down, so it will merge with the brown dampness.
She looks only momentarily at the clear demarcation
the envelope impresses upon the earth about it.
And then takes earth she's dug, a handful in her own hand,
and drops it upon the envelope. Just one handful,
and then without hesitating even an instant in the motion
she refills the hole, burying the red envelope quickly.

She does not make a mound, but flattens the place
with the back of the spade; completes the square with
grass originally removed. There are no flowers
in this patch, and there are no insects. But, fortunately
the grass is wet and green and a few weedy crabgrasses
are bunched towards the center.

7.

When she returns to the house, she goes again
to the kitchen and seats herself at the table.
Using the milk in the glass she wipes the soil
from her hands with the pale pink napkin, does not
seem to care about the dirt beneath her nails,
and dries her hands on the second napkin. The two
white envelopes, still unopened, have been placed
in the windows above the sink; the two broad windows
with the bright yellow curtains, where the lilacs
bloomed just outside.

Side by side the sun is glancing from them,
for it has become late in the morning. "I must
dress now, kitty," and she rubs the large yellow
head of the old male and pushes back her chair
from the light wood-frame table. She carries the cup
through the living room and up the back stairs
to her bedroom.

8.
The bedroom faces east, as does the kitchen, and
so the sun is throwing long slants of light through
the windows when she opens them. The trundle bed
is still mussed, and the heavy quilts have been thrown
to the floor in the night. The floral wallpaper
is delicate. Alternating red and pink roses in small
streams rush up and down the walls. First a tiny pink
rosebud, close and tight, followed by the bursting red
flower; halted then by the severe pink bud, clenched
exotically before a blaze of red rushes in once more.
Abruptly she turns from gazing at the paper, rushes
to the mirror and brushes her hair in short, rapid
strokes. She flings the bedgown from her and goes
to the cabinet beside the bed.

She chooses the red floral gown, the gown which
must be tied so tightly about the waist and bust that
she becomes the great red blossoms which mass and flounder
on the bodice and skirt. The sash is brilliant red
satin, and hangs in a long streamer down her back.
And her shoes are red silk. And her stockings a delicate
red knit full length.

9.
For the rest of the day she sits on the old swing
on the front porch. It is whitewash, too,
like the house; but it has green painted arms,
and creaks as she moves back and forth and she reads
until evening and supper.

10.
As the sun is setting and the cicada is receding coolness
coming she goes down from the porch and around the side
of the house. From the garden she picks two bell peppers,
one butternut squash, two ears of corn and two tomatoes.

She carries them to the house, and washes them
in the sink. She takes a very long time to wash them,
the two envelopes resting on the sill just above her.
She rubs and rubs the green peppers, and the tomatoes
and the squash, the largest of all; and then places them
and the unhusked corn in the red enameled tray she keeps
in the side cupboard for summer foods. She places it
in the middle of the table and seats herself. And gazes
at the colors which make up her tray of summer.
Not once has she dared go to the back of the house
to the place where the red envelope is buried.
But she does have courage to gaze now at the two white
envelopes: the one with thin black-inked writing,
large and bold, but not indelicate like that buried
in the yard; the other with thick curling letters,
with most of the address smudged out by some unnatural
means.

The yellow cat has come to sit beside her and is waiting
for his supper. She rises and goes to the refrigerator;
places before him first the dish of milk and then
the fish, with head intact for that's his favorite part.
And she seats herself at the table once again, picks
the tomato nearest her and begins to eat it without peeling
without the knife, the juice the seeds oozing down
the front of her robust dress.

11.
She eats both of the tomatoes and one of the bell peppers
and then abruptly leaves the table. The light is almost
gone, and a pink glaze is in the sky outside her windows.
The envelopes are turning pink, too, and the writing
and smudge leap at her through the increasing darkness.
She rinses her hands, ignores the damp redness of her
gown and rushes to the back door. The cat remains behind,
slowly washing his massive face, seated on the floor
which is deepening in color from woody pink to violet
as the sun sets.

Once again she goes to the shed, and tugs at the tools
lined against the wall. She is not careful, and does not
see which shovel she has. But it is the round one, and
the earth thrusts in spates from it. Brown, ugly clumps,
before it is too late.

12.
". . And so dear Elizabeth, I ask you this one time only.
And only this once. ." And she could never get beyond
this line. No matter where it appeared in his letters.
No matter whether he sent it by regular or by special
post. She could never read further with the great purple
ink rushing in torrents on the page, down toward the bottom
where he must leave off; and for all she knew, never
even finished the letter. Yes, it was the red paper.
The purple ink. How could he use such unco-ordinated
colors, so sloppy which ran so easily together and could
be mistaken one for the other? How could he send
the purple scrawl with such voluminous writing on such
a perfectly square red envelope. To her.

So, whenever the letters came, she opened the red envelope.
And she never got beyond this point. She would rise
from wherever it was she had seated herself to read
his impulsive letters; where she would come. .
No, she must be honest. She would seek out those lines,
which were the same in every letter. And she would know
that there was no change. That everything was the same.
That,

13.
And then she would bury the red envelope with its
purple request for one day. And in the evening
of that day she would unbury it; would place it
in the damp, mildewing pile with all the others
he'd sent and which she never answered.
And she would leave brown splotched earth on them;

she never brushed the earth from them.
She would close the old dresser drawer, and turn
out the light; would go back down the stairs
to the kitchen to try and finish her meal.
But when she got there, she could only gaze into
the dark, toward the unopened envelopes which rested
side by side on the window ledge for that one day.
And the red sore on her thigh would ache so much more
than usual; the purple creases of skin where its fibrils
apposed the chair would pulse so much more than usual.
And she could not eat another vegetable, or a piece
of fruit; nor would she drink the milk.
The yellow cat would lie beside her chair, and she
would sit in the dark and stroke him.
And finally, he would sleep.

INTERLUDE 1

". . That man's at the front door again.
    Yes. That's what I said. He's here
    for at least the fourteenth time,
    and the least you can do is be civil
    and talk with him. He says it's
    important. That he must see you
    in person to tell you.

    But why won't you go? Why!? It's such
    a simple, civil thing to do. You sit there
    (it's embarrassing, you must know it is. .)
    ask me to tell him you're not here   you're
    busy that you're not available or what-
    ever else.

    But what do you expect me to tell him
    this time? He's here to see you, not me,
    so don't try that again! I know you'd

like to be rid of it all, but you can't
expect someone else to take responsibility
for your   . .all right, but this is
absolutely the last time. Absolutely!
Do you hear me?   . ."

PART II

1.

Several times she had heard the sound in the night,
just beneath her bed, where the moonlight played
on the long floorboards. The cat would be there,
leaping down to the floor to catch it, whatever
it was; would bound about and would snatch
at the hem of the bedclothes. Would leap terrified
back up to gaze at her, full face, before all
his hair stood up and he screeched hightailing it
out of the darkening room. She would lie there
full of amazement from the wakening from sleep.
And would listen very carefully, but the sound
would not appear again. And the room was pitch
black. There was no moonlight at all, as she
had dreamed.

2.

At other times she would hear the rustling at her feet,
would feel the weight as it came onto the bed;
would open her eyes to see the wolf or the great
horned owl. Sometimes the mock terror was so great
she would see the Shmoo of Li'l Abner, rocking
right by her head. Rocking and smiling and moaning
in always the same voice the Shmoo would sing,
"I'm going to eat you up. I'm going to eat you up."
And she would notice that all of these visitors
were palpable, were touched by her; but would not

remove themselves, no matter how great her terror.
Would not recede, and that they always appeared
only when the yellow cat was gone, probably hunting.
Probably. And on these nights she was not ever alone.
Not ever.

3.
And sometimes she would awaken to the heavy breathing
of the man standing beside her, who had the kitchen knife.
He would say nothing, but would stand there and would hold
the knife straight down at his side; would breathe
harder and harder and would freeze her in the awaking
to find him there, the dark screaming and dry sweat rising
in her body. She would wait the whole night, the burning
in her body the whole night, listening to him breathe
and wait. Wait for the sun, or at least the first bird
to begin some sharp call or song.

This happened whether or not the cat was lying
on the bed. Whether the cat was near her feet or
at her shoulders, or had coiled himself about her head.
It would happen no matter what.

4.
And sometimes she would climb the stairs, and at
the landing she would look down to the dark wood floor;
would remember her brother standing on his bed,
naked, leaping up and down yelling and screaming
and saying how she would be gotten tonight how she
would be done tonight how she would be tonight.
And on these nights she would crawl in between the cold
blue-white sheets, would lie and would wait
for the bottom of the blankets to be lifted, for the hand
to begin caressing her leg; there, beneath the bed
the cold hand would lift the blankets and would touch
her over and over, never roughly but always in the same
way caressing her. And she would lie on her back,

rigid and cold and unable to move. Thankful when the cat
would lurch upon the bed, bringing the dead wet mouse
to her, dropping it on her face.

INTERLUDE 2

". . This morning she would make pies.
  Cherry and apple, perhaps lemon meringue.
  And she would leave them, after
  they were done, sitting on the window sill,
  beside the letters. There, where
  the lilacs had bloomed all spring
  and the small sparrows have built
  their nest for those screaming young ones.

  And she collects the flour, the sifter,
  the large orange bowl with sugar in a mound
  high above the rim; the lemons, the apples
  the washed dark cherries, the table top
  gleaming with the colors of her endeavor.
  And she scrapes the brown earth from all
  the red envelopes unburied and fills each
  with the great thick white meringue
  of all the beaten eggs and throws them
  into the oven where they burn
  with the thick sickening smell of blackening
  sugar filling the kitchen. And then she
  places the pies in the oven, too, and
  she lies down upon the clean bronzed floor-
  boards and sleeps beside the yellow male
  until she knows it is exactly time; and
  she rises up, opens the oven the great gas
  flame and places her bare hands onto
  the boiling bubbling innards the red blazing
  food yellow, places her head into the great
  open red and orange flame her hair and covers
  her with the dark ashes   burned   burned   burned

  And then she could forget everything.   . ."

PART III

1.
If there were a way I could relate this to you;
if I could tell you how it must have been, the quietness
the way the sun slants on the eaves. If there were
a way I could forget such things as sequences,
for she did not live by such timed events. I gather
you were able to learn some of this from the arrangement
. .or rather, the lack of arrangement, of things in her
house. Her bureau with her clothes, for instance,
lying along the sideboard in the kitchen,
except for the one red gown which she apparently always
hung beside her bed in the closet. Yes, I could tell
because that morning she forgot the sash, it was still
hanging from the lone hook inside. .yes, I am sure that
sash went with that particular gown as it was the same
color; and although badly burned, the loops in the dress
were just wide enough. And the fact that she never painted
the inside of any of the rooms since moving here over
12 years ago, while still wallpapering the bedroom
with those roses. And the cat, the big ugly thing
constantly underfoot during the investigation,
constantly merowing for some damn thing or another.
And the way she had "done herself in," as it were,
burning herself like that so severely over and over
and not calling anyone, and the face of her nothing but.
Well, we needn't go into it. It was she herself
who did it, there's no doubt about that, for she'd had
no visitors for over two years. Just mail deliveries.
The postman said she would receive, every month,
two white envelopes and one red. .   always on the same day.
The 23rd. We found all the white ones, but couldn't
find any of the red at first. It wasn't until the contents
of the oven were checked that we realized she had plastered
herself all over with the burning contents of what
she was cooking; and the ashes of the red enveloped letters
were mixed with it. We have no idea what was in those
red envelopes, but we know everything of what was in
the white, never opened envelopes.

2.
For each of 12 years there were exactly 12
white envelopes times two . .i.e., for each month
of those twelve years she was alone here,
she received two white envelopes. And all of them
were exactly the same—as pairs, I mean.

One member of the pair had a fluent fine-tipped
ink writing very elegant; while the other was smudged,
water-marked, nearly illegible addressing. The postman
said that after the first couple of deliveries he knew
exactly who they were for, so just took them there.
We found the most recent in the windows of the
kitchen, right above the sink, untouched   . .rather,
unopened. And we found all the rest in neat,
but not chronologically arranged, stacks filling
her dressers in her bedroom. None of these had been
opened except for the very first pair, received by her
on April twenty-third, nineteen hundred and fifty five.

3.
In the first envelope there was a white piece of paper
with a full-page pen-drawn face of a wolf, slavering
and with very mean eyes. Beneath it and partially
covering the lower part of the drawing was only one word,
"YOU" written in large writhing purple letters. .   not
smooth like the address was. The attempt at the face
of the animal was extremely ferocious, and would certainly
have scared a child. On the back of the page was nothing.

In the second white envelope with the smudgy lettering,
there was a white sheet which at first appeared
to contain nothing. But when we turned the sheet over,
we found, done in red pencil, like a regular marking pencil,
a large irregular dot. .much bigger than a period;
from which purple squiggly lines were drawn that extended
all the way down until the end of the page was reached.
It was messily done, like the word "YOU" in the other

letter, brusquely, emotionally. And in some places
the purple merged with the red in such a way
as to lose its own color and become that of the red
circle, or   . .yes, blotch is the best word. There were
no words written on this page.

INTERLUDE 3

". . Well, yes, we posted a man at the house
    after the remains had been removed. And
    we took the cat to the pound. We've
    been waiting, hoping there would be
    delivery of more letters. There was
    the present city postmarked as origin,
    but no more have ever come.

The postman's getting on in years;
    was pretty querulous but finally said
    he'd try and help. Would keep his eye
    peeled for any—red *or* white.
    We especially wanted a red envelope,
    but none of that sort have ever come.

Just one long rectangular business-like
    letter, about a month after; which,
    upon opening was simply verification
    of her seed order, placed the day before
    she came to her demise.   . ."

THE INDECIPHERABLE

YVES BONNEFOY

Translated from the French by Susanna Lang

I am walking along narrow paths which cross long wooded hills,
above a plain where, in the distance, a lake gleams, prisoner of still
farther hills. The afternoon is hot, the world seems empty in the
intense half-light of the olive trees and the pines; and yet, with
each step that I take, here the two pillars of a threshold emerge
among these leaves, or there a half-open gate: so there are houses
in this country; indeed, many houses, although each is hidden by a
turn in the drive which leads, I imagine, from the silent entry to
the front stoops, the double stairways, the low doors.

And I approach the plaques which have been attached to the
stone, or iron—but how difficult it is to decipher the inscriptions
traced there: usually such banal indications, in this summer coun-
try, where the names are so constantly the same, the signs so empty
of meaning. To begin with, the texts are long—real sentences; but
then these signs are obscure, confused, marked with words I do not
know—if they are even words. And it seems to me, too, that the
complexity is rapidly increasing: the first time, I had read, "while
one . . . another . . . and still another . . . ," among the moss,
the stone blackened in places; and if this phrase remained incom-
plete, had perhaps worn away, still it resembled a meaning, and
did not immediately fall from my memory. But soon the sentences
lengthened in the dark stone where they were carved, and became
endless, like the conversations of people obsessed, which you hear

sometimes through the wall, and which are lost in the noise of the apartment, only to begin again, alas! I am reminded, too, of litanies. Of archaic treatises on theology, which enumerated the contradictory and changeable attributes of forgotten gods and demons. Of the irrational or transcendent numbers of arithmetic. And if it were only the words! In one place, I thought that I could distinguish an illusion to the Celtic god "with four heads over one," a patronage remarkable even for the porch of an old church, but which you may sometimes find; unfortunately, this fragment of meaning was joined with crystallizations which seemed of another nature; you would think that these vowels or consonants had been combined at random, like the stones which are heaped, here or there, in the stream bed where the water loses itself. How much trouble must be taken, and for almost nothing! In these extreme regions of the Name, there are depths as in a ravine, where the sounding echoes are muffled, where you do not go; and at first because of the trees which tangle, almost horizontal, on the slopes.

Reaching for my pencil, and for the notebook I sometimes carry in my pocket in case I should need it, I undertake to copy the writing on a plaque which is suddenly here, before me, and which appears simple: a few lines, where the sun has brief sands which move, under the tree of the threshold. If I copy these sentences, it will be like a memory; I will be able to reread, perhaps decode them. . . . But this time it is the letters themselves which are the problem. The branches of this Y, for example, which I had thought could be easily identified, are each forked, in fact, and bent—broken and even doubled, several times, in strokes which rival each other, join each other, dissolve the symmetries which are a meaning: so that at the limit, once again in the infinite, I no longer know if this is a new alphabet, at the highest degree of formal complexity, or simply the trace, in this matter, of indifferent forces—crystallizations, erosions, explosions, blind hammers—which have made and now unmake what I call this place. Where am I? Is there any sense, now, in asking this question? With the mossy end of the pencil, I try to imitate on my page, which has begun to glow a little, these enigmatic figures, this presence which might be absence: but then the mark I want to speak again is cut into the stone—itself hard, or crumbling; and how can I repeat, in the black of my pencil, though it is hemmed with gray, this depth of the inscription, where the hand yet leaned with hope, and is still perceptible—who knows?—in the vibrations of the sculpted line; the hand which was the word? Ah, if color could be born there! If the color could blaze up, in this hiatus, like a fire!

Still I persist. What else can I do? I know that I engaged my destiny, long ago and without return, in this ravine with its high walls, and stony ground which leads into the distance, turning soon among the grass: the form—where meaning struggles, which everything denies, and the beyond, the obscure collapse, the depthless noise—matter.

HEALING

JANINE CANAN

I
I am living a study of the healing arts.
Feeling like a piece of shit. Psyche
and -ology are in controversy. Logic
whips its February winds. Strips every
acre arid. Oh barren. My orphan locked
on the ward, cuts veins to release a deep
fluent red. It runs down her whitecoat
onto the canvas. She likes to watch this
brilliantly vivid image of her distress.
Remember Charon, healer with the erupting
wound. Or the poet, who waits until midnight
to bind up her words. Or Mother who turned
and turned out all of the lights.

II
I am spending the night with women. One
each night. I have a nightmare after Carolyn
says the mugwort was wiped out by herbicide.
The mugwort that raises the dream off your
pillow to consciousness. In New York, I say
to Karen (we do not make love) when we go back
the garbage will be piled high as the skyscrapers.
I keep waking up. The skyscrapers are fragmenting

into personalities. In the nightmare the hall
is filled with dirty dishes. Garbage. I'll do
it, I say. Babygirl eyes. Pleading and the
piercing wind. Sherry and I go to the beach
and fall asleep by the hip of the ocean. Cling
like crabs to the sand.

III
I am spending my days at the ocean.
The walls are made of glass. Sunsets
play for me now in their gorgeous costumes,
pinks then oranges then reds.
I am standing in the sun drying out.
I am reading Anais Nin's last diary.
I am revising my poems.
I plan an endless series of portraits—
Ted, Helen, Carol, Bryce, Phyllis, David,
Andrew, Carol and Don, Peter, Beatrice, Paula—
who will one day take my place.

IV
Elaine says we are living in a chaos. During
dinner a darkskinned boy cuts the screen and
slides in. He takes the radio, father's white
jacket, my underwear, my mail, my address book,
my keys, my driver's license, my passport, my
ticket. My new black diary where I've sketched
a poem, "The Lesbian," that begins "A person
who cuts her hair when she is angry" and ends
"hard drinking and teething at her cunt." Will
he read it, stoned on my grass? Before throwing
out my postcards of the ocean, my rust wool bag
double crocheted by Irmgard to last forever,
Kate's handstitched bag with gold and orange flowers,
big enough to hold 100 afghan squares. Will his
girlfriend wear my Mexican pin: turquoise,
silverlooped, serpentine, depicting eternity.

Elaine and I are eating hot and sour soup. The
waiter asks us to leave. We haven't ordered
enough dishes. I'm worried about returning
without a present for Carol, the bone and wood
necklace I left in my bag. The mandala that would
open her heart. In the next restaurant, over
dishes and silver, Elaine shouts, No,
after asking her to bring back a jacket from Rio,
he never phoned again.

THIRTEEN DRAWINGS FROM THE NORMAN HOLMES PEARSON COLLECTION

Introduced by Aleksis Rannit

Do Writers Draw for the Right Reason?

Aleksis Rannit

1

Norman Holmes Pearson was teacher, literary-historian, essayist, critic; exponent and protector of H.D., Pound, Williams, Horace Gregory, along with many other poets; friend to New Directions and numerous national and international cultural institutions and organizations. When the news came that he had departed from us on November 5, 1975, it was impossible to accept. I hardly accept it now. That day, I recalled two things.

In 1939 I was asked by a once-famous Russian Futurist poet, Igor Severianin, to see that no date of death appeared on his gravestone, only his birthdate. Severianin died in 1941, and, alas, I was unable to influence his family not to use his death date. However extravagant his request, I think Severianin was right. The poet, if he has a true lyric power, cannot die. The death dates adorning the gravestones of Blake, Byron, Poe, Baudelaire, Whitman, Yeats, Pound, and others are merely corporeal. And what can those of Matthias Grünewald, Michelangelo, Tintoretto, El Greco, Goya, and Van Gogh signify for us who have eyes to see?

Contrary to Juvenal's assertion that the healthy intellect can live only in a healthy body, truly creative men through the ages have often suffered from bad health. Pearson was handicapped all his life, but his every day was marked by positive spirit, wit, imaginative conception, soaring flight, and growth. No, to paraphrase the ecclesiastical saying: he has fallen asleep in Apollo, but he cannot be dead. For Norman's friends, his death is only another state of his being, a continuation of existence under different conditions and with a different hypothesis, a "duplicate of life" as Swedenborg, whom Pearson admired in his youth, called the future life.

The second thing I remembered on that fifth of November was Maurice Utrillo's poem, of which he gave me an autograph as a keepsake in 1951:

> Tout ce qu'on donne fleurit,
> tout ce qu'on garde pourrit.
> [The things you give will flower,
> the things you keep will decay].

As a scholar and friend of idealist distinction and altruistic elegance, Pearson was that kind of giver of grace. By giving away "things," his time and his substance, freely to others, he endowed many of us with his intellectual and human "flowering."

Norman Holmes Pearson's principal hobbies were the collecting of first editions and the assembling of writers' drawings. In accordance with his last will and testament, his collections are now, together with his papers, in the Beinecke Library of Yale University. Pearson acquired drawings, manuscripts, and books not for prestige or because of snobbery, but out of devotion to and the wish to serve literature and the arts. For him the collecting, in and of itself, was an act of cultural significance. Even where other sources might fail to illuminate Pearson's personality, his collection of literature and art itself reveals his thought and taste, taste which did not fall victim to critical errors and partisan misconceptions but was based on aesthetic understanding of a number of different styles. From his rich archives we now publish twelve drawings by writers, the core of the marvelous and curious from this *Wunderkammer,* as the German critics used to call such assemblages. This series is graced by the virtuosic and reflective caricature-portrait of Pearson, in the style of the French *charge,* by the Estonian cartoonist and Pulitzer Prize winner, Edmund Valtman.

When speaking of double talent, as in the case of the writer-artist, one is puzzled in trying to determine which one of the two talents is reflected in his handwriting. Contemplating, for example, Goethe's forceful, painterly flow of ink, one may ask: does it document Goethe the poet, or Goethe the artist? The answer is damaging to the semiscience of graphology, for the handwriting reflects only the character of Goethe as poet. Goethe, the artist, who achieved a limited craftsmanship as a dry documentarist, lacked both the dynamic lyricism and the original vision manifested by Goethe the poet. Inspired by this conflict, we may well attempt to compare the style of these drawings from the Pearson collection with the literary convictions of the writers who made them.

2

Which of the authors in the Pearson collection achieved stylistic synthesis between their literary word and their visual logos?

Was it Victor Hugo?—Although in the Eliot era Hugo has been condemned, along with Shelley, Keats, and Swinburne, as "only a cheap sentimentalist," he was actually one of the greatest poets of his age, a *permanent* poet, to use the precise adjective cultivated by William K. Wimsatt. It is true that Hugo wrote far too much and that the quality of his work is uneven, but at his best he had a cosmic imagination and the capacity to make all objects come alive. Above all, he wrote in stanzas, not line by line, thus imparting to French verse an orchestral quality that it had never before had. In his drawing-stanzas, too, Hugo appears as a master of the metaphor and a master of orchestration. Since 1891, when that remarkable exhibition of painter-poets was held in Paris (in which Gautier, Merimée, the two Goncourts, and others were represented by their more or less important works), the world has known what a gifted draughtsman and powerful dramatist in landscape this poet was. Today, he cannot be passed over in the history of landscape drawing. Even in his reminiscences of nature—spirited and suggestive of graphic color—drawn with a rapid hand, the fiery glow of Romanticism breaks out. But then, he was not only a Romanticist; many of his castles, citadels, cathedrals, and other buildings, as in the masterpiece in Pearson's collection, show him as a pioneer of modern architecture. Did Le Corbusier not see Hugo's drawings before he started to realize his own style of architectural design, which in itself shows Hugo's characteristic features, such as the raising of a building free of the ground.

Was it Mark Twain?—I pose this question in play, but seriously as well. Twain never studied art formally, although, as an organic talent, he was, potentially, an artist. As a writer he is commonly considered a humorist and is without a doubt a humorist of remarkable comic force and refreshing fertility. There is no lack of mood in his sketches and drawings as well, and, as in his prose, there is never a hint of affectation. Twain, the artist, doing the work at hand instinctively, was very likely unconscious that he, as a vigorous *naïviste,* was making a certain contribution to the art of black-and-white. In his drawings there is not only humor and pathos, character and truth, there is also a largeness of outlook, something we find, for example, in the more dramatic lithographs of Daumier. Thus beneath his fun-making we can discern a man who is fundamentally serious and whose ethical standards are well established. Twain signed his sketch, now in the Pearson collection, as an "educated artist," probably with reflexive irony, or perhaps he was asserting that he had a command of a truthful and direct style of drawing, as well as supreme command of vernacular American English.

Was it Bernard Shaw?—Shaw, who received some training in painting at Wesley College, Dublin, was an accomplished draughtsman. He left behind thousands of pen and brush sketches. In his plays and their renowned prefaces, Shaw is a spiritedly stimulating writer, gifted with Swiftian irony and a mastery of clear and witty prose. In his visual art he gave us the same social satire, the same unconventional philosophy and rhetorical speech, and brought a new intelligence to the mastery of graphic line. Because of this, Bernard Shaw's work, as that of an experienced artist, is, technically and stylistically, almost equal to his plays. One of his famous sayings was: "You should live so, that when you die, God is in your debt." Art critics are definitely still in his debt.

Was it Paul Valéry?—Valéry's most beloved subjects at the Collège de Cette were philosophy, drawing, mathematics, and later, art history, especially architectural theory. In addition, his aunt, the Impressionist Berthe Morisot, believing that Valéry's talent was that primarily of a painter and not of a writer, strongly encouraged him in his artistic efforts. The poet, however, considered himself only a

"Sunday painter"; yet he practiced etching, painting, and especially drawing, all his life, his finest studies being a series of almost surreal glove-compositions. Valéry devoted most of his art-time to architectural drawings, feeling that architecture was the greatest of all arts. His Roman sketch, *Piazza Cavour from My Window,* is an example of his poetic realism. Soft and delicate lines prevail, and the central qualities of his poetry—the search for ultimate cognizance, for geometric asceticism, and the "delirium of lucidity"—are absent, as in all Valéry's other drawings, watercolors, and paintings known to me. Contrary to his literary works, which are the acme of intelligence and manifest a love of measuring the meridians of inner experience, Valéry's visual creations do not indicate the value of philosophical meditation or even demonstrative formalist economy. And although speculative quality is sometimes there, it cannot be compared with the immense power of radiation and the full aura of suggestion which mark Valéry's art of poety. *Piazza Cavour* is, rather, an instinctive lyrical piece. In his verse, however, Valéry showed an unwavering mistrust of the spontaneous and an interest only in the spectacle of the mind's functioning.

Was it Marcel Proust?—Proust's drawings are rare, and it would be difficult to build up an aesthetic theory about them. Nevertheless, the finished sketch in Pearson's collection is an aesthetic statement, as well as an exaggerated and mysterious portrait of a Decadent whose theme is the quest and conquest, by "unconscious memory," of the external values hidden in a temporal world. Proust's literary style remains unique in its complexity and its affectedly erotic beauty. The same can be said of his exquisite mannerist drawing, attesting to the author-draughtsman's taste for psychology as an end in itself. Does Proust afford his *Fuad Pacha* a sufficient reason for living or a romantic manner of not living?

Was it D. H. Lawrence?—An interesting episode in Lawrence's life occurred when, in 1929, an exhibition of his paintings was raided by the London police on the grounds of indecency. But, as Matisse pointed out to me with his Gallic exactitude in 1951 (in Vence, where Lawrence died): "The only amoral work of art is a bad work." A compelling, red-bearded man who electrified those who met him, a man often gently sweet but sometimes violently angry, Lawrence was a legendary figure in arts and letters, and the subject of many hectic memoirs. His late work, the *Portrait of Arabella [Helen Corke],* the only portrait of his known to us, shows that he never lost confidence in his "demon" and pursued his artistic assays with gusto and sensitivity until the end.

Was it Hermann Hesse?—In his literary work Hesse treated themes taken from his own life and spiritual struggles. Influenced by Schopenhauer and Nietzsche, medieval mystics, the teachings of Buddha, and the ancient Chinese philosophers, he combined the romantic dreaminess of a Decadent and a weary Art Nouveau writer with a deep undercurrent of disillusionment. But none of this is present in Hesse's watercolor, *View from Montagnola*. It is done solidly and optimistically and carries explicit reference to the strong sensations of light, form, and space. That characteristic, delicate odor of decay which rises from the soil of Hessean prose is missing. The geometric landscape, earthly and heavy, bears rather a certain resemblance to Picabia's and Delaunay's synthesis of crystalline and round-shaped Cubism. The use of purely optical phenomena applied here as compositional elements makes a strong impact on the viewer. Yes, the *View from Montagnola* was not painted by Hesse the writer, but by Hesse the celebrant colorist, a painter of singular architectonic gravity.

Was it Henry Miller, the perennial Bohemian, whose rhapsodic works achieved a candor that made them a liberating influence in mid-twentieth-century literature?—His free and "easy" literary style is commonly reflected in his bold drawings and watercolors, full of primitive impulse and sensitive emotionalism. Miller is one of the most honest experimental artists of the twentieth century, and his self-portrait shows a probing for the inner person beneath outward physical appearance. Its symbol is the horizon: always receding, never attained. Without being demonstrative it evokes a grandeur, as well as the transcendentalism of the so-called Gothic world of expression, which rejects the classicist Italian conventions of harmony. And yet an animated new harmony is present as a combination of delicate and precise linear drawing and spontaneous flow of color. Both as a writer and an artist, Miller produced work of deep breadth and full voice. Instead of pleasure in the object, pleasure that enlightens or transfigures, there is now in American arts, thanks to Henry Miller, a torment from which respite must be won if life is to be born.

Was it Jean Cocteau?—Cocteau's work shows a range of flamboyant diversity, and, of all the writers, he, like William Blake, is probably best known as a poet-artist. He is in every art-form an individual versemaker *and* artist who explored the eternal human themes—love, escape, mystery, magic, death. A skillful and subtle draughtsman, he reveals the pathos and sadness underlying his assumed mask of gaiety. Cocteau is an artist with a quick sensitivity, and the fluid expression of his forceful drawing-greeting reproduced here must be intimately linked with the style of his literary work. He surprises his readers and viewers, knowing how to convert the acrobatic and artificial elements of his overingenious egotism into a beautifully natural, elegant gesture and his highly cultivated mind into pure lyricism. Cocteau called his own drawings *poésie graphique,* but we may well describe his pure, unornamented poetry as obsessed with the melody of graphic line.

Was it e.e. cummings?—In the 1920s and 1930s cummings divided his time between Paris, where he studied art, and New York, his literary headquarters. The eccentricities of his mannerist poetry were seldom convincingly reproduced in his drawings and paintings which were exhibited in several one-man shows. As a bizarre transcendentalist, he did not create a school out of his stylistic innovations (he himself, his typographic arrangements and punctuation included, was, in part, a follower of Mallarmé and Stefan George). As an artist he is, in general, a master of premeditated style. It is interesting to note that in his watercolor *Silver Lake, New Hampshire,* in which he expresses the vitality of an Abstract Expressionist, the aesthetic loveliness of open form stands in contrast to his poetry. Judged by the standard of his poems, *Silver Lake* lacks classicist form and structure, but it has undoubtedly, in full measure, the romanticist qualities and merits that the artist sought to give it. Might not this watercolor be placed next to a dramatic page from cummings's expressionist drama called *Him?*

Was it Rosanna Warren and Susan Alon, two younger poets in Pearson's collection?—One may call Warren, who has been published in national reviews, a cognitive poet for the manner in which she converts her experience into contemplation, in the psychological and aesthetic sense of the word. She is a disciplined, self-contained lyricist, and thus there is always an emotional coherence beneath her intellectualism. These qualities are well expressed in her drawing *Olive Tree,* in which mechanistic vision opens the way to a tectonic suggestion of deeply elegant rhythmic motion and coherence.

The poetry of Susan Alon, the author of two collections (*Bells and Clappers* and *Saturday Night the Duck Threw Up*) demands close attention because it relies on metaphors that are concerned not with logic but with the associative significance of words and with their psychological nuances. Alon's verse, impetuous and consciously unrestrained, is much freer than her art, perhaps more supple, but brittle, too. *The Good Man Nutcracker* reproduced here is, nonetheless, a fine example of the poet's strength as an ardent artist. It conveys a direct rendering of feelings and emotions, expressionistic in a sense, but without violent exaggeration or distortion.

3

Norman Holmes Pearson liked to call his collection of writers' drawings "art for the wrong reason," but he admitted, also, that "sometimes wrong and right reasons are coupled." Was it wrong of Goethe, who defined himself as an "eye man," *Augenmensch* (a term changed, by Colette Inez, brilliantly, to "eye-theist"), to spend many years of his life trying desperately to become an artist?—His preoccupation with drawing and painting not only helped him to create his color theory but also helped him, as a poet, to sharpen his romantic and classical visual perception. Something similar could be said of Valéry, who developed the sculptural and linear quality of his verse as a result of a lifelong, intense preoccupation with fine arts.

There is a misunderstanding in the critical approach to some true artists: Hugo, cummings, Hesse, Miller, Shaw. Too often it is said: "They are fine writers, and they paint, *too!*" But if they had kept their practice of visual art a secret and exhibited their work under pseudonyms, they would be discussed in art histories, in place of many second-rate artists who are taken seriously. Conversely, the poetry of such artists as Michelangelo and Raphael or the belletristic criticism of Van Gogh and Matisse—under like conditions—would invariably be studied by the historians of literature.

I am not very hopeful, however, that this may happen.—In his splendorous manner, Hugo drew gloomy seas and dark unearthly shores, fairy palaces, proud citadels, and cathedrals of fabled story, and I am simply sketching my own little dream house.

Edmund Valtman. *Portrait of Norman Holmes Pearson, A Friendly Comment*. India ink drawing, 13″ × 16½″. 1974. Inscribed: "For Aleksis [Rannit] affectionately Norman Holmes Pearson," undated, and "Aleksis Rannit'ile sõpruses Edmund Valtman 11. aug. 1976" [For Aleksis Rannit in friendship Edmund Valtman August 11, 1976].
Photograph by Joseph Szaszfai

Victor Hugo. *Mansion at Seashore*. Sepia drawing, 6½″ × 9½″.
1842.

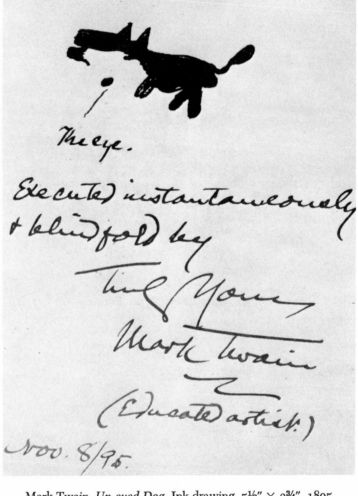

The eye.

Executed instantaneously
& blindfold by

Truly Yours
Mark Twain

(Educated artist.)

Nov. 8/95.

Mark Twain. *Un-eyed Dog.* Ink drawing, 5½″ × 3¾″. 1895.

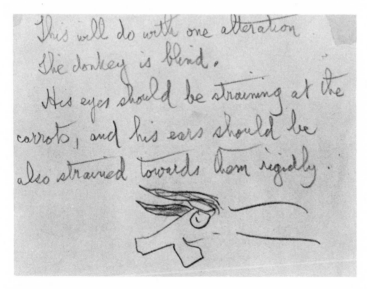

Bernard Shaw. *Self-portrait as Don Quixote*. Pencil and watercolor, 6¾″ × 9¾″. The accompanying note, pencil, 3½″ × 4¾″.

Paul Valéry. *Piazza Cavour from My Window*. Black and reddish pencil with white wash, 4¾″ × 6¾″. 1926.

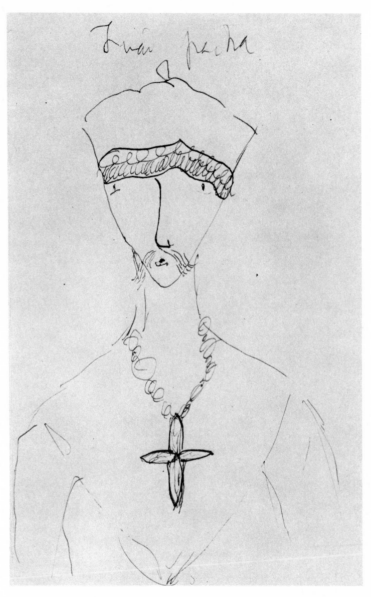

Marcel Proust. *Fuad Pacha*. Ink drawing, 6¾″ × 4½″. 1919.

D. H. Lawrence. *Portrait of Arabella* [Helen Corke]. Watercolor, 19½″ × 13½″. 1916.

Hermann Hesse. *View from Montagnola*. Watercolor, 9½″ × 12½″.
1936.

Henry Miller. *Self-portrait*. Pencil and watercolor, 18″ × 13″. 1928.

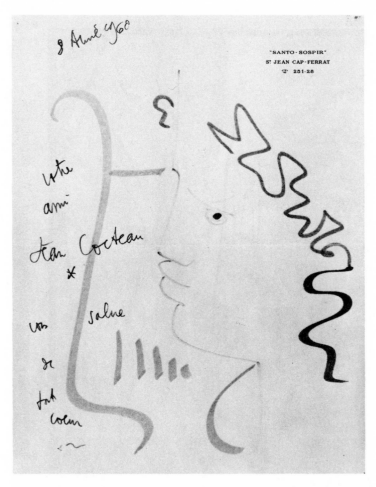

Jean Cocteau. *Greeting*. Pencil and watercolor, 10½″ × 8½″. 1960.
Inscribed: "8 Avril 1960 Votre ami Jean Cocteau vous salue de
tout coeur" (April 8, 1960 Your friend Jean Cocteau greets you
wholeheartedly).

e. e. cummings. *Silver Lake, New Hampshire.* Watercolor, 11½" × 17½". 1930.

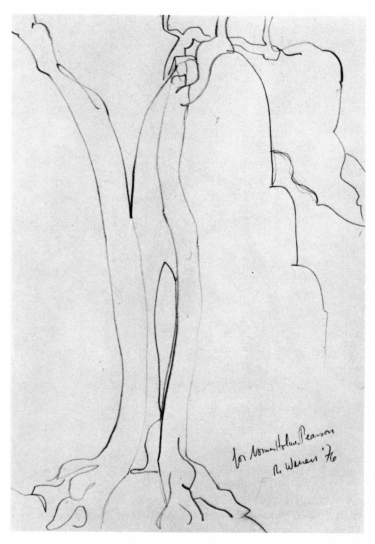

Rosanna Warren. *Olive Tree*. Pencil drawing, 8¾″ × 6⅛″. 1970.
("'76'" means: Yale class of 1976.) Inscribed: "For Norman
Holmes Pearson. Rosanna Warren."
Photograph by Joseph Szaszfai

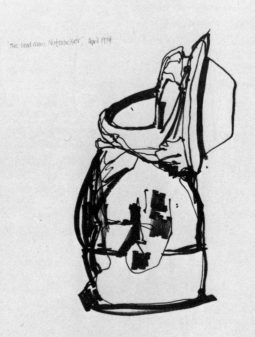

Susan Alon. *The Good Man Nutcracker*. Felt-tip pen drawing. 7¼″ × 4¾″. 1974. Inscribed: "For Norman Holmes Pearson / a friend of peers, in distance myself, / unmet not unmarked. Susan Alon."
Photograph by Joseph Szaszfai

THREE POEMS

WILL STAPLE

SIERRA LOVE NOTE

empty high sierra cabin
one room, table, bench
    a note on a nail
by the one window
      "the day you're due
    I rise before dawn
if I know you'll be here at 4
I'm already happy at noon"

such a lighthearted tenderness
      erotic and trusting
    —you love not when you wish
      but when you love—
when you're older it's no different
    it just takes longer.
dance partners, hold not tightly
but confident in the same pattern
      move
intricate   swift   gaily free
    no grasp   or clutch
      nor clinging arm   heavy hand
    but held somehow, invisible
save the barest passing touch.

SOMEONE ELSE'S TOUCH

when a man lives the lie he has to live
to lie with the woman he loves
is he still worthy of that woman's love?

when his touch does not excite
as much as she thinks   someone else's touch
would excite   should he touch her?

should he let on
            that the thrill is getting gone
or should he simply savor
            that sad sweet bit of pleasure
pretending nothing much feels wrong?

MALE CHAUVINISM PRAYER

                        join in the fight,
brother, for individual dignity, not selfishness, and if you are
really brave you will choose your adversaries from those who hold
the potential for the greatest pleasure and reassuring care—

            o Lord deliver me from bitterness, deliver me from the
            body felt rage the head swims in recalling how deeply hurt
            —recalling how there are no curers except in the camp
                    from where my enemies have wounded

            o Lord it is not just women and gold,
                    i would prefer to be two months old and to have a
                        most
                    wonderful mother warmly to care for and nurse me,
                        with fullest love,
            o Lord i would not cry
                            or pee too much in my pants.

MY GARGOYLES

PAUL WEST

As I remember it, being fourteen corresponds to the role of the movie extra, secreted within the thorax of a fake triceratops which threshes about in automatic combat with yet another triceratops within whose thorax yet another extra earns the same pittance. The dumb alias promotes, but, watching the film of such a primeval encounter, the youth within may well feel failed: the death agony of the loser is colossal; the brute strut of the victor imbecilically huge; the blood, rich devil's-lava; the soundtrack, daunting feral thunder. Yet, one youth's tummy aches, the other's head. The mastodon masquerade cannot last for ever, or even for long. The bravura shrivels and the know-how dies a natural death even as it impresses. At least, that was how I myself felt at such an age, when I fell short of heroic impostures expected of me, wishing I were instead an opossum. Bravely enough, no doubt, I tried to pass muster with bats and balls and the gear of other rigmaroles whose ancient honor ruled me along with millions; but dealing with girls was a surd altogether beyond me, calling for a masterful agility I never had and do not even pretend to now. I made the attempt, though, imperfectly rehearsed animal that I was, and just hoped against hope that *Homo sapiens* had been designed both first and last for books, airplanes, and chemistry experiments restricted to flasks, pipettes, and Bunsen burners. As I probe, the maladroitness of those wincing years stays put, at a convenient distance, does not come through entire. Something in me shrinks still from what I could not do, or, doing, did ditheringly wrong. Rose-cheeked

95

Sylvia F., with whom I lay innocently in the deep spear grass during one clement English August, snaps out of view because a red ball has clicked against a fudge-brown bat. The delicate and hypnotic birthmark which, aslant her cheekbone, gave Betty G.'s green eyes a starry, catechistic elongation, vanishes into the pall under a bomber's cambered trunk. The double ping of the thumbbell on June A.'s bicycle (which triggered off aortal tinnitus in me) drowns itself in drab black gunpowder on a round filter paper, no competition for sulfur, saltpeter, manganese dioxide, and potassium chloride (this last the stuff that made the bang).

Banned by pastimes I found vocational, these and other girls mix a fata morgana in my head, even now: lovely periphrases that call up Latin fairies and fates, Arabian coral (*margan*) and Greek pearl (*margarites*). The intense brooding I did on them in my tender years pays off now, fleshed as a heat-trembling frieze of tireless eidolons whose expression, a joint constant between winsome huff and roguish pout, eggs me on to make up for time not so much wasted as stilled. I was unspeakably slow in the accost, though with palpitating heart I did in the long run establish a regular movie date with Sylvia F., in ninepenny seats on the apocalyptic back row of the Rex cinema; go to Betty G.'s house on her birthday with, as gift, a record of Bob Crosby's Bobcats' raucous version of "The South Rampart Street Parade," which she detested on first hearing; and hold June A.'s magic bicycle for ten minutes while she entered the chemist's shop (in search of gruesome stuffs I pruriently thought a goddess should not need); we talked in blanks until she flashed off with a downthrust of her lissom thigh. They are all three still flashing away from me a quarter of a century later, seachanged into varicose viragoes (I guess), awaiting the first hot flash. Not that it matters: I long ago projected their hesitant elegance, if such it were, on to Keats's Grecian urn, that *ronde* of paradisal halts, and they abide at the ready, primed for an attention that has not come until this very moment.

Squeezing memory until it yields or snaps, I should be able to particularize these girls through talks or outings, but little or nothing sounds, recurs. With their physical immediacy unimpaired—Sylvia F.'s flushed calves (sign of poor circulation, doubtless), Betty G.'s small-stepped chopping gait, June A.'s habit of tossing her head back as if she had long instead of cropped hair—they nonetheless remain incomplete, have been definitely extruded thus by a memory that usually behaves much better. All three are silent, with no captions evincing their minds' movements, and I wonder if, here of all places, I have not a sample of what I remember only too well: an adolescence without conversation, when the answer to the throwaway question, *What's new?*, was always an unsaid, *Only what's ephemeral,* with no one half as eager as I to chat about such unfashionable "dry" things as Kinglake's *Eothen,* Maupassant's tales, Eliot's poems, compulsory reading that had switched on big searchlights to my moth of mind. Of course, my teachers, who after I reached fifteen were all women (because no self-respecting male taught arts or humanities), responded as best they could, and a brilliant, unstinting response it was, edged with repartee and spiced with an occasional cigarette in the teachers' common room. They were just too busy, teaching seven hours a day, to hear out the verbose importunities of their only male pupil (for, by the same token as the male teachers went, no self-respecting boy specialized in anything but sciences). Out on a limb of grimy *finesse,* while my peers hacked away at the trunk of the tree of knowledge, I developed a peculiar and incurable sense that the arts, literature, even philosophy, were disreputable distaff pursuits and that I was a nascent freak.

From that period, I recall only one conversation, keenly morbid on my part, with a boy named Gerald Roberts, who informed me that he was going to have to wear glasses. At once he became an object of endless conjecture, for all the world as if (to lard an anachronistic analogy into my recall) he were due for a heart transplant. His future looked invincibly prosthetic, deliciously marred; one of the limping wounded, he might soon be dead or at least insane, and with shuddering relish I envisioned myself likewise bespectacled—walled in by glass aureoles in ogive ribs tricked out with golden wires like a crudely repaired mannequin—and deemed it a fate worse than death. Obsessively I questioned him about the testing he had undergone: the optician's card that shrank from bold-face roman capitals to quivering minuscules; the scalding eyedrops (which reminded me of the potion—quinine and phosphoric acid—fed into me for a month, a year or so previously, for my incessant nervous blinking); the selection of the frames and the tiny

catafalque that held them safe. Did looking through the lenses
hurt? Were the glasses heavy on the nose? Did he feel that people
could less easily peer into his eyes and read his thoughts? Did he
feel shielded? Unwittingly, Gerald Roberts, myopic rabbit to my
Frankenstein appetite, had given a face and a name to an unthink-
able abomination; it was like being affable with the condemned
man while the hangman pinioned his wrists above the drop.

I still back away from the release of pent-up morbidity that boy
set off. I must have been inordinately terrified by myths of mutila-
tion, grounded no doubt in some excessive regard for natural
beauty, or at least for God-given orthodoxy (a kind of Christian
Science esthetics), and fomented by Saturday afternoon movie
matinees in which, from behind a screen of ribbed protoplasm, The
Clutching Hand came flexing out, sheathed in an eerie surgical
mitten tipped with two cones of horn, on behalf of an owner—The
Phantom of the C.H.—whose ruined face one never saw for a sort
of sinus mask, with a cord trailing down. The Phantom of my
callow psychodramas not only had an acid-eaten face and a rat-
infested lair in the sewers; he had first twitched to composite life
strapped to the operating table of Dr. Frankenstein-Jekyll-Moreau,
who not only harnessed the lightning but rendered the final mon-
ster both vampiric and lupine, hunchbacked and intermittently in-
visible, Cyclopean and dragonish: in brief, a ghastly dysgenic col-
lage which, at home, sent its carmine, serrated maw after me as I
ran up the cellar steps with a jug of milk, and out and about waited
for me in alleyways, trashcans, and derelict air-raid shelters with a
live bat between its teeth.

A version of this *thing* still dogs me at the moment of falling
asleep and even during the day whenever I allow my eyes to blur
focus and so free the retinas for spontaneously generated ogres of
a mind disjoint. Just as easily, innocuous images arise, free-floated
from a cerebral marina which, if cut, would gleam softly like so-
dium: a pair of silent dogs, a setter and an Airedale, on a dim,
brittle autumn afternoon, trotting through leaves in a steep wood-
land, like two itinerant seniors paroled from some canine moun-
tain clinic; or a brain-damaged boy who whoops fiercely as he
whirls through the air inside a tire roped to an overhanging bough
that just must not break; or stratocumulus at sunset, when low
water clouds of dark Indian red hem in what resembles a levitant

ram of weathered chalcedony. These images I welcome unreservedly, uncaring what they mean. Observe, reader, how I have just flinched from setting down the features of my private demon, whom I long ago began to call Areemayhew, a verbal ricochet from my first years of speech when, I think, the word or phrase stood for something I soon learned not to mispronounce. Yet those four syllables lingered on, a gross quotient, a husk of lugubrious phonemes, reserved for the troll of my mind's eye, seen like this: enormous-pored tanned skin with white pig bristles jutting high from ruptured follicles; pupil-less lavender-blue irises in unlidded purulent whites flecked with blood like certain yolks; teeth the hue of wet straw and abominably rotten, like one of those mock-ups that dentists site within view of the chair. The entire head is wet (the white hair looks like dulled magnesium ribbon), whether with perspiration or rain I have no idea: it could be that of some dead and long-exposed forest ranger, or some Amerindian-Nordic feat of miscegenation. Less certainly, for I never have more than glimpses of certain other features, I think the nose is aquiline, the nostrils are capacious. Of ears, eyebrows, I see nothing, but the neck looks unhandsomely weathered.

Thus Areemayhew, whose manifestations forebode nothing, whose face corresponds to that of no human I remember, though it evokes hundreds. I have occasionally willed him to appear, and up he has lurched like a herald of plague or bloodcurdling delirium. The cremation of my father, in his seventy-fifth year, has come and gone, but it is not my father's face, although I suppose it could be read as an augury of that event, and certainly functions now as a vestige. In any event, before he went to sleep never again to wake, my father told my mother he had "just had a wonderful day, a marvelous day," and I cannot square that beautiful closing asseveration with my inscape's ghoul, to whom I attribute no consciousness at all. Areemayhew, warning of who knows what, replica of none, symbol of naught, I prefer to regard as the product of such a process as the block portrait which reduces the face of George Washington, or the Mona Lisa, to six hundred twenty-five squares, thus eliminating details that one may partially restore by viewing from twelve feet away, or making one's head tremble, or jiggling the picture, or by squinting just a little. I am more than willing to pigeonhole Areemayhew as what Thomas De Quincey called an involute, a compound experience incapable of being disentangled or forgotten, a perdurable enigma raised to exponential maximum, and all the more intimidating for being the face of *someone*. So far, it (I hover between *he* and *it*) has not literally petrified me or changed me into a salt monolith, dolmen, or menhir. If it is not Vincent van Gogh, seen by the light of an oil lamp, it must be a dead prospector in the Sierra Madre (Walter Huston, perhaps), with both of whom I have inchoate affinities. "He that fears leaves," runs one of Mallarmé's thousand *English Sentences to Learn By Heart*, "must not come into the wood"; but I was born therein; there is nothing to be done. Priggishly addicted to orthodox beauty, I subconsciously prepared for an appalling letdown by fixating on variants all the way from poor four-eyed Gerald Roberts to the long-armed, gloating Nosferatu of Max Schreck. I dolefully resented my mother's having to wear glasses: they made her more distant, more of a wire-and-plastic construct; I hated the spring-driven clop of her spectacle-case, and even the clammy fluff of the cleaning-pad beneath its lip.

Anyone diagnosing in this child a severe case of precocious perfectionism, a hyperesthesia beginning with an eye-maimed father created by an exploding shell in 1917, will have a point. Saved from a certain amount of sharpnel by the blood-soaked corpse of a man later identified as one Corporal Blood, my father no doubt instilled in me, through the hour-long war stories I foolishly never wrote down, a sense of the violence that can be done to man's flimsy symmetry. Apt pupil that I was, I held his dry, well-manicured hand, and tried to look into his unseeing left eye, where the wound's tiny white scar twirled in the dead iris like a worm.

Less dismal folk than I, or he, have invented much more horrible figures than Areemayhew. Medieval craftsmen, who could not read and had received no training except as apprentices in a stoneyard, fancied unconstrainedly in face of the incomprehensible, coming up with gargoyles that evince the forces in us which make us frightened of ourselves. That is why we have, and accept, these eidetic waterspouts, as if enacting century after century a line that Hermione utters in *The Winter's Tale:* "The bug that you would fright me with, I seek." Awesome phenomena of Nature personified, they originally took the form of dragons with live animals in their mouths (foxes, pigs, rabbits) or, as in the *papoire* of Amiens, a man inside a wicker effigy, operating monstrous jaws, or, as in the spiked and spine-serrated Tarasque of Tarascon, several men, who shot out fireworks. Such prototypes belong among ceremonies of blatant license, when sausages and dice rolled on high altars, priests wore grotesque masks, the laity dressed themselves as monks and nuns, asses came into church, and the congregation brayed. Amid such good humor (part of it, but not quite), folk burned cocks and hanged pigs, stretched all kinds of animals on the rack in order to read "confessions" in their cries. It was some eschatological levity that relished such an assortment as Virgil Tied-Up in a Basket, monsters under the mineral feet of depicted saints and bishops, both the presentation of dead souls as nudes (nudity being seldom used for other purposes) and of the damned as head-bellied, head-breasted, pelvic-winged, toad-vomiting epileptics. In those days, piety eructated, vice was a bit of a wag; beasts of the field knew right from wrong, and honest men sanctified their own dung. Since then, I think, we have become unjustifiedly simpler.

One's notion of gargoyles, at any rate, is almost always too strict. There are leaden and wooden ones as well as those of stone, symbolical ones and not. Some are not in the least bestial or even sarcastic. There are as many monks, nuns, pilgrims with staffs and wild men as there are animals and birds. According to Mrs. Jameson, they have their origins in prehistoric Silurian remains dug up in the Middle Ages, whereas others have discovered in them Isaiah 13:8, in which the sucking child plays on the hole of the asp and the weaned child sets his hand on the adder's lair, with equal safety; in Psalm 21's "mischievous device" and Psalm 22's gaping mouths and "I am poured out like water"; and in the bestiary of the constellations. Emile Male declares them of no symbolic force whatever, but of homely, spontaneous birth in the imaginations of housewives listening to primitive tales during the long winter watches. But, of course, there have been many who claim a church's every stone has a meaning and that gargoyles represent devils conquered by Light and enslaved for menial chores. Or they derive from processional animals or from those griffons of the East which, in ancient lore, stood guard over treasure. Call them what we will— all the way from those choked by molten lead from roofs in two world wars to the stunted cherub, Charles Laughton, among the "nightmares" on the towers of Notre Dame de Paris—they upset, provoke, fortify, and unquestionably display the dark (or dark-daft) side of man's presumed unconquerable mind. Even the drolleries on the misericordes do this, as much in the age of Dachau as in the Middle Ages. All very well for the Aristotles, Horaces, and Doctor Johnsons to inveigh with suety worthiness against freakish phantasmata: there is another view, less exclusive and more historical, which remembers how beauty is the cutting edge of terror, that art invites us to entertain childish responses we fight even as we indulge them, and that much of our gratitude goes to those great creative invalids whose madness—in print, stone, paint, music, dance—forestalls and partly precludes our own. After werewolves come Roger Bacon's talking head, *Titus Andronicus,* Walpole's *The Castle of Otranto,* Jack the Ripper, Bram Stoker's *Dracula,* Dr. Caligari, expressionists of all kinds of mutilatory persuasions, P. T. Barnum's Feejee Mermaid (a hoax monster, shriveled, a yard long, with hideous teeth and a fish body sewn to the head and hands of a monkey), and the yawning or screaming disemboweled (although also partly disembodied) figures of Francis Bacon the painter, who is never without a textbook entitled *Positioning in Radiography.* Our monsters will not save us, of course, but they tell us what in part we are, suffering on our behalf, turning night into day instead of the other way round. Adding enigmas, horrors, freaks, of his own making, to those inflicted upon him by the universe, we remedy nothing; but, in fighting back no matter how impotently, in rehearsing time and again this metaphysical protest, we deepen our sense of hubris. Or so I believe, being of the chimerical persuasion since a few years old. Only recently, I pasted a mask over the face of John F. Kennedy in my reproduction of Robert Rauschenberg's collage, *Buffalo II,* troubled by the cliché status of that face, which Rauschenberg put in before the assassination. The horror resides in the mask now, as in that overexposed face it no longer could.

Unable as I am to resist any gargoyle (the essentially unliterary stamp of the genre wins me over every time), I still play favorites. Accordingly, among gargoyles (and using the word in its widest sense), as among souvenirs, I recur to about a dozen. The face of the Tarasque of Tarascon is that of a proptotic, teeth-gritting Negroid feline. In a mouth at Reims, the tongue extends to the bottom of the jaw, as if tugged out too far to be retracted, its shape that of an egg. At Bayeux, a single-headed, double-bodied beast of the thirteenth century grins with eyes closed, like an impossibly affable archdeacon flying blind toward us. Cut into the buttresses of Notre Dame de Paris' transept and sacristy, south side, pantherish gargoyles project like slim, underslung turbine engines. At Josselin in Morbihan, there are two bizarre figures not easy to forget: a wild man, with corrugated pelt and the lion-face of the leper, shoots horizontally from the wall, baying downward, an attenuated Burl Ives, and a dark-hued monk, in the jaws of an equally dark monster, looms like a tumid penis, fed by one gutter and two connecting spouts. In an arcade in the Toulouse Museum, dozens of abstract figures bark upward from stone perches, like so many circus seals, arrested in mid-yelp of unappeasable stone hunger. A simian fetus at Ploare, in Finistère, turns its sea monster's eyes upon us, but the right one wanders away to catch what might be round the corner. A Troyes nude, her entire face arranged round her clamant mouth, kneels astride her plinth, seeming with one hand to rip her ear away. An amorous frog chortles, hand on heart, I do not remember where. A flying Jonah tries to yank his ankle and foot out of the whale's mouth. An enormously-genitaled satyr croons for his supper. A monk with a face created decomposed, rather than in stone that has broken down in the meantime, puffs up his cheeks and appears to orate diagonally down from the roof. One pigtailed harridan's throat grows all the way down into her frontal spinal column, which ends in a sigma-shaped tail. A one-headed jackal is devouring a man's head, whereas a three-headed one (variously) gapes, repines, dozes. A prow figure, a realistically carved alchemist who might be a fugitive from a Disney movie, aims his gaze across and above the roofs of Paris, as if waiting for them to melt into something thick and strange. Five heads in a row embody, left to right, blasé porcinity, rubber-jowled gullibility, grieving reticence, shocked submission, and canine astonishment. No competition for Areemayhew, they compose nonetheless a stunted symphony in which he figures as a compatible goblin. Thank goodness he has a tribe to which to belong, flesh though he is to their flawed stone.

Bodiless, he truly belongs among the heads which, trunkless by design, fill the upper corners of bell towers, stand on columns at portals, grin in the leafwork of friezes and tympanums, doing nothing mild by halves, whether they happen to be bat-headed totem tops or the archetypal Nobodies dear to allegorists. Cockeyed and slew-mouthed, anonymous heads rise before me in undulant echelon, urging, *Myrres vous y:* See yourself here. An outstanding one in Reims averts its eyes from a seeming elephantiasis of the nose and lips, its whole expression bulbously forlorn. Another in the same cathedral has a face dart-sharp and ascetic, honed on pain, as if some "pear of anguish" (a torture device which expands the mouth) has just been withdrawn; indeed, the teeth in the lower jaw look cropped, while the upper is blank. Other Reims faces enact the gamut of deformity all the way from such mild "bits" as the cheeks insucked about some oblivion-giving sweet (or in histrionic dubiety), through such a middle-of-the-road sample as the jaw-locked Neanderthal guffaw, to the prolapsed yawn flanked by vast polyps that dangle like overstuffed sausages from either side of the jaw. I weary just a little, I confess, of the lion-faced subhumans, as of importunately grinning monks; and it is the charred, macerated-looking heads which take the firmest hold on my flighty brain, evoking all manner of atrocities photographed in black and white. Here and there a bagpipe player or a leaden angel varies the mode, reminds me of a life customarily savored or an afterlife promised on cheaply printed leaflets thrust into the mailbox in all weathers, or, like that cowled, abraded, becangued head in the stairway of Rouen Cathedral, hints at a unique and unknown life form, this time in deep space, incommunicado out of choice. Its darkness is not Stygian at all. A brilliantly chiseled Snail Man teases my mind with slow-motion claustrophobia, from which a mother baring her child's backside for spanking returns me to an earth which can exhibit, alongside Samson and his lion, at Reims again, a window sign that reads, "Tripes Bouillon Portions À Emporter." After the farmer killing his pig, and the bee-faced vegetable seller, I am almost ready for Areemayhew, to whom no social customs matter, for whom there remains only a vegetal declension into talc-soft inoffensive moss.

Then the inevitable happens. A strong aroma of garlic-and-chicken stew flirts with my nostrils. A letter from the Bahamas arrives, its hand-canceled stamp flying the blue-and-yellow flag, with black triangle inset, of Independence, above a shrunken porticoed mansion that has the vulnerable aura of an artillery target.

A friend telephones, reminding me to see the film of *Death in Venice*. Unparaphrasable busyness invites, and I—who in the mind's unlinear Hades was phoenix and centaur and Ancient of Days, reaching with flail-shaped proboscis for a moon shaped like a radar dish, or battling giant rabbits, or debating in a forest with chimerical birds, or eyeing a sixteenth-century Suzanna in her double bed among the Elders, or marveling impartially at two nude men glowering at each other over a low table loaded with apples or gourds, or at turtles with angel-heads—I lose eschatology, extremes, that whole hinterland of invincibly inert madness, and once more trail the grating fiber-pen over the canary-yellow paper lined with arsenical green. I am thankful for a good stomach under a correctly aligned cage of ribs.

In the end, the frightful images both in and upon those venerable cathedrals lose their smack, and reassure almost as much as the comic scenes from medieval daily life. The phantasmagoria is mainly human, after all, and even its devils have a diminished, Pyrrhic force alongside the baneful fruits of yet another investigation. Copied into a small notebook manufactured in Baltimore, on several of seventy-six sheets four inches by six, I have innocuous-looking sketches of various bacteria: *Mycobacterium tuberculosis,* like the fork-twig of a rudimentary catapult or an old Phoenician letter *f; Streptomyces* species, a similar twig, except that from one arm of the fork depend three strings of tiny frogspawn or berries, a 7 between a 6 and a long 11; and *Corynebacterium diphtheriae,* a troop of shapes which includes tiny black-tipped dumbbells and warped Indian clubs. Amazingly, these miniatures can take us off, as can those called *Vibrio comma,* little gherkins tipped with a curly whisker, which cause cholera; *Diplococcus pneumonia,* like a halved nut with a kernel in each of two separate compartments; and the one with the forbidding name, like a drum roll in snow, *Treponema pallidum,* whose tight spiral, like that of a stretched-out typewriter ribbon, brings syphilis and yaws. When I first copied these awful six, I thought: they belong where the gargoyles are; *they* are the enemy, out of whose long-invisible doings men superstitiously concocted ghoulish surrogates. Then I realized that gargoyles are an art form, whereas bacteria, despite the art in their forms, are givens, *données,* facts: tokens of the intricately inventive and revered emeritus nothingness which medieval cathedrals made substantial, like zero signs in stone. I was, quite traditionally, confusing man with God; but no man yet made a bacterium, no god carved a misericorde, unless all man's creations belong to his gods as the spin-off of divinely given potential (a slavish credit I will not endorse). No worldview, I told myself in that slyly epiphanic instant, should be without either gargoyles or bacteria; but, where the bacterium is fixed, the gargoyle is a delirium in free form. That is how, in the long and fatiguing run, universe lost out to *poiesis* in my little notebook of unseemly sketches, and loses still, no matter how far we may be from synthesizing a shagbark hickory, a home-grown *Vibrio comma*, a Jersey cow. Our retaliatory totems, gross as can be, underwrite sleep, sanity, and all the incongruously doomed love on the so-called darkling plain.

Among terms coined by military men as part of idiomatic anaesthesia, "god-botherer" for chaplain makes better sense than most. They reasonably (for them) suppose that one ought not to pretend one can pester inaccessible divinities; better by far to look after the men's welfare and provide the apprehensively dying with any kind of placebo. God-botherers bother everybody but God. I can see, now, how I might have become one, informally, by extending cosmic disappointment into divine accost, or rhetoric into putative influence, even to the point of saying to the First (or Subsequent) Cause, as if to a literary or a tennis acquaintance: "Do not so readily assume that whatever friendship there was between us has survived your recent crass behavior." Spurning such egregious mouthfuls, I know only what the gargoyles know, in all their miscellaneous stuntedness. Half-inclined to side with them (and Areemayhew) against all variants of heroism, all marriage-minded teenage girls (whether beautiful in hindsight or not), and all bacteria (given a job to do, they do it), I find myself doting on something lovely in the grotesque, whatever its forms: gargoyle, gurning, Halloween, the two Lon Chaneys mugging with violent humility, Max Ernst's railway compartment in *Une Semaine de Bonté*, in which ravaged-looking traveler looks away from both the bare-legged corpse on the floor and the great, spiny, glaring, overanimate Sphinx at the window. Beyond the straitened face of the norm there ripple the endlessly mobile features of initiative: Clio with an expressive set of masks.

Sylvia F. disappeared into a sanatorium, struck down by *Mycobacterium tuberculosis*, and for a month or two I walked about the village and the school inhaling mighty cliff-top breaths to quell whatever had been puffed across; I did not plan to die of any such thing, not with a chemistry set which, properly exploited, held the cure for every ill, although exactly how the Gershwin purple of potassium permanganate crystals would merge with the green ferrous sulfate and dusty pumice-gray lumps (strontium nitrate) that glowed in the dark, to make a panacea, I was unsure. To the purple salt that dyed, disinfected and deodorized, I added the green one that was both pigment, fertilizer, feed additive, and water-purifier, fervently willing that the addition of my third chemical (a mildly radioactive lava, after all) would transform the mixture from something that brought the color back into those cheeks and calves, massacred her minor germs, enhanced her aroma, made her at one stroke pregnant, voracious, and pure-watered, into something that necromantically besotted her with the young alchemist who pined, lovesick, over crucibles of acrid burbling mud. All that remained, I thought, was to pass a current through the mixture, then send her a registered packet that held the precipitate: send it anonymously, "From an ardent admirer in the laboratory," labeled, with complacent pith, in unreadable "doctor"'s hand, "To be taken once only, before retiring." I never sent it, of course, part of my problem being the slapdash, generous mode of my chemistry and my word-builder's rather than scientist's attitude to formulas. I can recall one travesty, which went as follows: aluminum sulfate, plus tannic acid, plus ferrous oxide, or $Al_2 (SO_4)_3 + C_{76} H_{52} O_{46} + FeO$, which astonishingly yielded not a compound but a phrase: A FOOlS eCHO 3. Thus, even at thirteen and fourteen, I made puzzles of a low order out of Creation's building blocks, even as, a quarter of a century later, I find myself, sometimes whimsically, sometimes with an almost scientific impulsion, appropriating for my own fictional purposes the cosmic bizarreries called quasars, red shifts, and black holes. Sylvia F. declined in an unheated hospital full of scarlet blankets and inhaled an air cold enough to make her eyes pour.

Failing her recovery, through the ministrations of experts (I having withdrawn mine at the last moment in order to concentrate on the creation of a pyrotechnical device I might sum up as a radioactive roman candle), I would accompany June A. into the chemist's and there purchase, by the gross, provender of inhuman masculinity, so as to make things clear once and for all—and whoever wanted to could steal her unattended bicycle. As it happened, June A. disappeared too, into a domestic science college a hundred miles away, there to become proficient in meringues, Yorkshire pudding, and Scotch eggs: hardly a science, it was domestic enough to be learned at home. Exit June A., then, blithely pretentious, doomed to reappear in an ostentatiously colored college scarf, which she would flaunt around the village as if just down from Girton College, Cambridge. But, through some compensatory miracle, Betty G. became one of my mother's piano pupils at a shilling a lesson. With cramped-feeling chest, I watched her arrive each week at the front door, unseeably from my third-story window, then listened with almost servile approval to her scales and elementary pieces. When my mother rebuked her for some malfingered chord (which was not often), I froze, marveling how Mildred West, graduate of London's Royal Academy of Music, could be so undiscerning and cantankerous. At my boldest, I interrupted with a cup of tea my mother frowned at, needing none, while I blushed and redundantly hovered to catch Betty G.'s inflammatory eye, promising myself (oh, furtive voluptuary!) to nose the aroma of the padded throne she sat on before the next ivory-hammerer arrived. And it is with that vibrant nasal afterglow of hay, warm rubber, and silky asafoetida that she begins to go out of my life, a blissful damosel whose acorn-mind already knew how many infants she would have, what hue curtains in each of her house's rooms, which type of calendar (agricultural rather than Foreign Views) she wanted on the walls. In the year I went away, she won a gold medal in the Advanced Grade of the Royal College/Royal Academy examinations, a feat which gave my mother a long sustained smile like a twenty-four-hour bloom. But Betty G. did not like Bob Crosby's band, or being too near the sea or me, and I was happy to go away to fresh impostures.

Beauties in those days were like dandelion clocks: one blew their fluff away, muttering extinct formulas. Monsters became the most intimate companions of all: oneself at one's worst, in inspissated extremes, and Areemayhew gradually came into his own. As for the silence, it was like that before and after gigantic blasts of the Boston Light Ship's foghorn, a steam-drive diaphone that shatters downtown glass. At seventeen I found people to talk with: too many, in fact, for the good of my freshman studies. Out came the squashed-down romanticism. Minor exhibits on my chamber of horrors degenerated into the trivial: dancing, Christmas carols, schoolgirls with imitation engagement rings; puppy-love letters endorsed BOLTOP (meaning, of course, "Better on lips than on paper") or SWALK ("Signed with a loving kiss"); virility cults; the albino verse of P. B. Shelley; English damp, English coins, English fun. After six months of untidy bull sessions over coffee, beer, and cider, I realized that much of adolescence had dropped beyond recall, while its polarities—jussive abstractions of painful ecstasy and ravishing ugliness—stayed put, indispensable as systole and diastole.

Fatally afflicted with urbanity, I reckoned my very heartbeat allegorical and told myself that, at least until head grafts, things would stay this way. Extremes, not streams, of consciousness I envisioned as I ploughed into *Beowulf*, the poem with the Great Divide down its middle. All those half-lines evoked half-lives, contrapuntal opposites, Pisces (which folk jubilantly told me I was) swimming in two directions at once, purgatorial igloos whose underhalves accommodate no one at all. I was so glad to lift head above the pubertal compost that I almost forgot to strike up conversations with the nervous, industrious scholarship girls, whose mitigated simpers came straight out of Jane Austen's novels and their brains from the mint of heaven itself. Unbeautiful they may have been: box-jawed, myopic, mat-haired, stone-gaited, and nailbiters all, they nonetheless gave the morbid me a glimpse of self's yellowish rough diamond, just a touch lustrous in its blue kimberlite matrix.

SIX POEMS

JÁNOS PILINSZKY

Translated from the Hungarian by Emery George

TWO PORTRAITS

Brontë

The coachmen send word: we're coming.
And the guests: we're arriving.
And, flying, the lamps
slice through square and courtyard,
gilding the night,
the walnuts' trunks, the vines'
petticoats, and the stone table's
rain- and wind-dipped rim.

So, then—we're here.
Open the door.
This is our closing night,
our final visit.

Set the table.
Make the bed.
Stack the stove.
Let the dogs loose.

Rembrandt

Paternal house: of ashes and vinegar.
Kiss and handkiss: of ashes and vinegar.
Eyes closed in grave and in bed,
in an attentiveness beyond death.

A PAST HALF-LIVED

For Ted Hughes

It arrives, grows rigid,
sits on the cinder-mute wall:
a single, enormous blow—
the moon. Deathly silence its stone.

It shatters the roads,
it shatters them—the moon's light.
And tears the wall in half.
White pours down on black.

Black daylight lightens,
lightens and lightens.
White pours down, and black.
You are combing your hair in the magnetic storm.

You are combing your hair in the gleaming silence,
in a mirror even more alert than a half-lived past.

You are combing your hair in a mirror, speechless,
in a glass coffin.

GAME

Leaning over the green felt-covered table
it's my dead father.
But what is it that he leans over?
And what, just what does it want;
what is this lit-up,
caved-in gravesite,
this solitary game, this
man-back saying?

Let us not, don't you, disturb the backs
of his held-out right and drawn-back
left hand, and the alertness, the
ratio of the cue suspended
between three balls.

After all,
ball and cue darken,
halt without me, without you as well,
and with them I too halt, for whom
this game now goes on,
now, and forever.

VAN GOGH

1
They undressed in the dark,
embraced and fell asleep
while you, in the brilliance,
wept and considered.

2
Dusk was falling.
In the precarious heat
the sun came paper-close.
Everything stopped.
An iron ball stood there as well.

3
"Lamb of the world, lupus in fabula,
I am burning in the vitrine of the present tense!"

A LITTLE NIGHT MUSIC

Bouquet of Flowers

O gallows-fragrance!

Dialogue

Let me in; I'm here;
open the door; I've arrived.

There's no door we could open;
no bolt that could shut you out.

Midnight

They roll away in the unknown silence,
deep under the stars
they roll away
and stop,
the motionless billiard balls.

Mozart

A house, a courtyard. My dream and my death.
Southern silence, memory.
Searchlight-gleam on the walls,
emptiness and marble veins.

"Dans cette maison habita Mozart"—
Mozart lived here once.
In a vase a bouquet of flowers.

O gallows-fragrance!

ELYSIUM IN NOVEMBER

The time for convalescence. You stop in your tracks
in front of the garden. Your backdrop is a quiet
yellow wall's monastery-silence. Gentle
small breeze starts from the grasses,
and, as though anointed with holy oil,
your senses' five tortured wounds
feel relief and healing.

You are shy and jubilant! Yes,
with your limbs, translucent as a child's,
in the overgrown scarf and topcoat,
you are just like Aliosha Karamazov.

And you are also like those tame ones,
those who resemble children, yes, like them too,
and just as happy, since you want nothing anymore,
only to shine in the November sun,
and to be fragrant, light as a pine cone.
Only to warm yourself, like the blessed.

ANTONIO SALAZAR IS DEAD

JAMES MCMANUS

ANTONIO SALAZAR IS DEAD

Dona Dinora opens her thighs and begins soaping her labia, sing·
ing to herself about nothing, as is her custom, at the top of heɪ
lungs. She scrubs her face with a washcloth, then washes her abdo-
men, in back of her ears, under her armpits. She scrubs and shaves
and daydreams and sings. She shampoos her hair, takes a brush to
her back and her feet, rinses herself off.

Clean again, she stops singing and gets out of the shower. Two
men are waiting for her in the bathroom. One hands her a towel,
the second points a black M–10 at her cheek and tells her to put
up her hands—that she is under arrest.

"For what?" asks Dinora, raising her hands.

"For the murder of Francisco da Costa Gomez, Mario Suarez,
Vasco Goncalves, Antonio Ramalho Eanes, Antonio Salazar, Antonio
Rosa Cotinho, Alvaro Cunhal, and Otelo Saraiva de Carvalho," says
the man with the gun. "And put down that towel."

"But Salazar is already dead," says Dinora, dropping the towel.

"We know that," says the man with the gun.

Dinora is dripping, goosebumps have formed on her, and she is
getting ready to shiver. Her hands are still raised, the towel is still
on the floor. There isn't a single thing Dinora can think of to say to
these men. That she could sing for them now isn't even considered.

The man who had handed Dinora the towel now slaps her across the face, twice, first with the back of his hand, then with the front, very hard.

"We already know that!" he says.

YOUNG SEVENTH-WORLD WOMEN

One Wednesday evening, in the middle of "Starsky and Hutch," a small group of young seventh-world women knocks on my door. There are six of them, their perfect skins range from dark ocher to beige, and I am impressed. Once inside they begin removing their bizarre looking costumes—all very deliberately, too, an article at a time, each, I can tell, showing off for me as well as for the others. I'm unable to stop them. Stripped down completely, then, they march as a unit into my living room, their exquisite seventh-world jewelry glistening in the bulb-light.

To be on the safe side I examine their passports and take each of their fingerprints, asking them to have a seat while I run off some copies. I also bring in three extra chairs and pass around two boxes of mints to help keep them occupied.

When I return to the living room, I introduce myself and ask the women why they are here—naked, this far from home, and all sitting crammed so tightly together on my living room couch.

Five "didn't know" and the sixth is obviously lying when she says she was prospecting for feldspar deposits in the neighborhood and "just decided" to drop by.

To break this impasse, one of them suggests that we try some friendly tag-team wrestling, them against me. I think about this for a second, then cautiously accept. As soon as I do they're upon me.

Two incredible hours go by.

Finally it's midnight. One by one, the women begin to get up, make some excuse, and start getting dressed. I personally show each to the door; each thanks me for my hospitality and gives me a light peck on the cheek. Not one of them will actually leave, though, until I've firmly stamped her passport and handed over all four copies of her fingerprints.

"But how," I ask one, "did you know that I'd only made four?"

"Special Earth-resources technology satellites," she says. "How else could one know?"

She's out the door and down the stairs before I can get a really straight answer. I decide to forget about it.

At last only one of the women remains. Naturally I assume she'll be wanting her documents, too, so I go off to my safe to retrieve them. But when I get back she is gone.

All that's left is her national costume lying in a heap on the floor: a single piece of teal-blue silk, three mauve polyester scarves, some unexceptional panties, and a pair of silver high heels. I can't help picturing her now, either, walking by herself in the dark without this national costume, and I rush out into the night to return it.

All six women, however, are waiting for me downstairs in the lobby. They're now wearing identical maroon kneesocks, plaid skirts, and blazers; brandishing pistols with silencers; and laughing hysterically. One of them produces a white plastic handcuff, and they place me "under arrest."

In silence now, they lead me outside, where a huge limousine is double-parked with all of its doors open. I also notice that none of the street lights seems to be working.

"Where are we headed?" I ask, and the handcuff behind me is only drawn tighter.

TORQUE

Tuesday, and I'm in The Gap again, hawking straightlegged Levi's and smoking the last cigarette of my life: my pack of Old Golds is now empty, and I've vowed never to buy another one. An attractive young woman is in one of the dressing rooms, trying on a pair of my pants, and I'm watching her through one of the three two-way mirrors in the office, passing the time while I wait for the manager. I'm also listening to Brubeck and Mulligan *Live at the Berlin Philharmonic* on the tape deck. The manager will be back any minute with his own pack of cigarettes, so this will be my first big chance to test my resolve.

Unhappy with the first pair she tries on, the woman begins push-

ing the stiff denim jeans back down over her thighs. As I watch
her struggling out of them, I fall somehow into a kind of half-lucid
reverie: I imagine that the fate of the planet's four billion people
hangs on whether I can toss the empty pack of Old Golds into the
wastebasket. The wastebasket is next to the doorway, about eight
feet away; although the edge of the manager's desk blocks my
view of half of the rim, the toss is quite makable. It has to be me
who makes this toss, it has to be made from where I'm already
standing, and it has to be done *on the first try*. All the rules gov-
erning the toss, it seems, have been specified by "a U.N. committee
assembled especially for the occasion." I'll be forced, for example,
to stand behind a thin purple line in the blue carpet's pattern
which is being monitored by a beam of light; if broken by my shoe,
the light's circuit will automatically trigger the destruct mechanism.
If I miss the same thing will happen: the entire planet will start
falling apart a continent at a time, according to alphabetical order,
then explode into space. Africa, I realize, would be the first land-
mass to go, then, though not by that much.

Across the polarized glass from me, the woman is casually testing
the elastic in her panties and fiddling with a thin silver chain she
wears looped twice around her waist (and from which, I notice,
nothing is hanging). She appears through for the moment with the
trying-on process, but not about to go anywhere or get dressed
again, either. The toss, I decide, will be dedicated to her.

I am ready, sweaty palms and all. At my imagined request, "The
Sermon on the Mount" has become the designated background
music. My second request, though, for one final cigarette, has been
denied by the committee.

Weighing the pack in my palm, I find it heavy and well-balanced
enough to be accurate with. Everything is set.

I breathe deeply and toss as I exhale, thinking, All the good luck
in the world can't save it now . . .

From the beginning it looks like a basket. The pack, however,
manages to graze the edge of the desk top, then caroms about
thirty degrees off its arc and falls out of sight . . .

But the committee sees everything; they have the whole toss on
videotape and will need only a second or two to issue their findings.

When I look back in on her now, the woman appears to be
staring straight into my eyes. Her sweater is pulled up and she has

both breasts cupped in her hands, kneading them like bread dough while tweaking herself on the nipples. Instinctively I lower my gaze and hold in my stomach.

The committee's findings are that my toss hadn't been as accurate as they'd hoped, but that gravity had helped force the pack back on course; special Earth-resources technology satellites tracking its flight had determined that wind resistance was also a factor as the pack had begun to uncrumple. All this can be seen in the committee's slow motion replay. In the end the pack had been able, the desk top notwithstanding, to just catch the far inside of the rim of the wastebasket, poise there for a second, then topple back into it.

The manager of The Gap returns to his office at exactly this moment.

THE EYE OF HUNAN

Hunan, Kham Ping's young son, is knelt in the gravel before her. It is announced he is guilty of attending a school in the city. Using the legs of his great-great-grandmother's table, three Khmer Rouge soldiers begin clubbing Hunan to the ground. Kham Ping is restrained by two others.

During the beating, Hunan's left eye somehow pops out. Noticing this, one of the soldiers calls for a halt to the blows and kneels by the body. She picks Hunan's eye from out of the gore, rolls it around on her palm, then deftly tosses it up to Kham Ping—who, in her daze, accidentally-on purpose manages to catch it.

Inside her hand, what's left of the eye does not proceed to sprout wings and soar heavenward. It teaches no one in the city to see, for it cannot see itself. It does not reveal to Kham Ping any secrets. Nor does it disintegrate into a vapor, scalding the hand of its mother. It does not teach the soldiers a lesson.

For two days Kham Ping wanders the deserted streets of the city, clutching the eye of her son.

THE SHACK DWELLERS

An *asalto* was in progress on a hill around the corner from a row of shacks somewhere in south-central Mexico. Two Mexicans were taunting a gringo, purposefully shoving him around, and laughing. "Ha ha ha." The gringo lay in the dirt, cut, and with a case of bad diarrhea; he'd run out of doxycycline two days ago. He still had his money, but his vacation was ruined.

Mr. Vesuvius, a rich Costa Rican, interrupted advertently. "Boys, come now," he said. "Iron this out as guests in my sumptuous shack compound why don't you."

To this the gringo was very amenable, but the two muscular shack dwellers were not. Misconstruing (on purpose) the idiom, they did to Mr. Vesuvius what was almost bad Spanish for "iron out," then laughed. "Ha, ha ha ha. Ha ha."

To avenge himself, Mr. Vesuvius unsheathed his *machetazo* and with eight quick chops neatly severed the head of one of the Mexicans. Mr. Vesuvius and his bodyguards then bolted into the foliage. The remaining Mexican was stunned, mostly by the sight of his best partner's head wobbling around next to his shoe.

The gringo saw his chance now and took it. He, too, bolted, losing himself on purpose in the row upon row of shacks and crud, not stopping even briefly to play kick-the-head with the Mexican's head, as Mr. Vesuvius had.

The Mexican who still had his head buried (temporarily) both parts of his partner, then returned empty-handed to his shack to face his small starving family.

His young wife was nursing a starving infant; her breasts were opulent and full—unlike her small *jacalucho*—but their milk just was not all that nourishing. The Mexican gazed down at the two of them.

He and Jesus, he told her, crossing himself slowly, had failed to relieve a cruddy mick gringo of his dollars then kill him so that he could not go to the police on them then, blah blah blah. Interference also was called on Mr. Vesuvius.

The beautiful wife, on purpose, said nothing. It was too hot for talk in their shack now.

When siesta time passed, the Mexican took off his shirt, propped up his toes on a stool, and began a set of seventy-five diagonal

flexiones, laughing in time to the strain. "Ha *ha,* ha *ha,* ha *ha* . . ."
He was still in a mild state of shock.

His wife looked purposefully on.

From the cuffs of the Mexican's trousers, six bronze coins made
the short drop to the soft dirt floor of the shack.

The brisk, useful exercises continued.

THE SKINNER

For a second offense, Bernadette's sentence is light. It's only The
Skinner. To help prevent backlogs, such sentences are executed im-
mediately. Bernadette removes all her clothing and enters The
Skinner without having to be dragged, then lies down by herself on
the smooth aluminum table, facing up. The door closes behind her,
out go the lights.

Right away she is frozen electrically into a spread-eagled posi-
tion. Not one muscle can move. Two surgical blades begin moving
upward from the tip of each middle toe, slicing through Berna-
dette's skin at a depth of exactly two-seventeenths of an inch. The
Skinner does not make mistakes. At the same time, a third blade
begins where the first two will eventually stop, a point midway be-
tween Bernadette's two lowest ribs and her navel. This blade moves
up her chest, throat and face, automatically following with sonar
Bernadette's personal topography, and ends by parting her scalp to
the rear of her cranium. In the meantime, blades four and five are
working their way down from the tip of each middle finger toward
either end of her collarbone, where they'll head for her throat.

Next, twenty-six pincers (they are not unlike alligator clips)
fasten themselves at regular intervals along both sides of the five
seams of skin and begin parting it. The pincers are programmed
to peel the skin back quickly but carefully, so as to cause neither
undue suffering nor rips.

Despite these precautions, Bernadette is now in some pain, so a
syringe is raised from the table and a small dose of morphine is
administered into the base of her spine. Since speech is impossible
for one being skinned, The Skinner itself must determine both the

drug and the dosage, as well as if and when a painkiller is necessary to begin with—but not once has it failed to do so correctly. About two quarts of Bernadette's blood have also been lost, so a transfusion of plasma is given. Again, the required amount is determined remotely by The Skinner's own delicate sensors.

Once her skin's been removed, the current is turned off and Bernadette is helped from the table. Two nurses apply a special petroleum salve, in order to prevent further blood loss or shock, then help her get dressed. The Skinner prints out a prescription for Darvocet and codeine to relieve the normal discomfort once the morphine wears off. It also suggests that Bernadette wear all-cotton clothing for eight to ten months.

Fully convinced now not to do any more of whatever it was she was doing before she was sentenced, Bernadette is free to go home to her family, to grow a new skin, eventually to return to her job—and to start, it is hoped, an entire new life for herself.

SEVEN POEMS

GANGA PRASAD VIMAL

Translated from the Hindi by Millen Brand and Rattan Chouhan

THE NOONS OF SOHNA

An indolent mountain
is sprawling.
The sunshine shifts from the heads of the laborers,
lingering on the leaves and the trees.

Sohna is rich in flowers,
green
grassy lands,
air,
and the rocky plains.
But there is a citadel,
a relic left there by the past.
Peacocks cry endlessly,
shrilly.
When the sun shines at
the top of your head,
the farmers grapple with
the indolent expansion of the fields.
This has been going on for centuries.
Where there was a jungle
there's a piece of cultivated land.

Where there was wilderness
there's now a home.
The noons come and go, every day
fondling
the small trees.

AT THE THRESHOLD OF
THE ARAWALI JUNGLES

That journey
is like a faint recollection.
There lurks
not the terrible eye,
only time hung on
silence,
a patch of cloud
looking at the sky.

No sooner does a door open
than a spell is cast.
The opulence of nature
is scattered, as disorderly
as song being misplaced.
How difficult it is to fold up
a memory,
and it is equally impossible
to recollect it continually.
At the threshold of the Arawali jungles
some far-off
horseman is standing
like a statue.

AN INTIMATE TALK WITH A FARMER

This is a plow,
This a spade,
this a piece of land,
this a barren cow.
This is my family—
ignorant kids,
a woman sticking to the fireplace.
Dear sir,
It's quiet in your city,
but my stomach,
see,
it's India.

OLD TREES ASSOCIATED WITH GHOST STORIES

Old trees. Having borne history
for such a long time,
you have grown lonely.
This actually happens. A vague belief
eats into you. All the same
your stories hide you graciously
the way your bark
hides your hollows.

There are words. Countless.
That had been current
from the earliest time
but have been discarded
in our time
like rulers.

Indolence. Oblivion.
It's the hallmark of history.
I will continue to carry

the relics.
Old trees. What remains is only
the air that imagines your glory
and listens to you
and the sky that does not look down.

There's a world of difference
between us.
You wear a few seasons, just a few,
and we,
centuries.

SEASON

I had seen him
standing in the backyard.
He was calm and quiet then,
composedly gazing at the trees.
He stayed in this silence,
watching how an old man
sinks in the shadows.
And how an old man
signaled to him and ran toward him.
He remained bent down for a while,
then straightened himself
and walked everywhere along the city avenues.
He raised his hands up
to show that he had won.
I saw him afterward climbing the trees.
On the one hand he unveiled the eye of the seedling,
on the other he blindfolded the towns and villages.

THE THING THAT REMAINS

I often feel
that I am the only page
that time has spared.
Others have been heaped
with dust.

Scattered particles of dust
blur names.
I often feel
that I am the only name
that hasn't been covered yet.

There are friends
and relatives.
There are so many eyes
and such a great expansion,
but time after time
I feel
I only have been spared—
a shrunken day.

There are countless faces.
There are countless assignments for them
and for those who are blindfolded.
The ratio is the same
for those who despite their sense of sight
haven't seen
the thing that remains in isolation,
the thing that knows me
and despite knowing
deserts me at intervals.

THE DAILY ROUTINE

February. Spring is still
asleep in the arms of
the sky.
A glimmering ray
will herald its advent
and will toll in advance
the end of the cold.

At the furthest point
where snow still covers the green,
wind
with its infant cries
wakes up the valley.
At the furthest point
where infant fingers shiver,
there an eager smile
gladdens the dates.

From morning till evening
day wears on in its routine
and, the day after,
eyelids close
in the arms of the sky.

COSMETIC INSTRUMENT

HARRIET ZINNES

She is standing far away from the spot on the couch where the wine had spilled. The red wine, a weak Beaujolais. On the white couch. She is standing in the far corner of the long living room. She is standing far away from that corner couch. She is looking at that couch. Will she get rid of it because of that single deep red spot? Because of the spot? Or because of the history of the spot?

She is not looking at the spot now. She is sitting. Sitting at her desk in the upstairs bedroom. She is alone. She is holding a pen. She is asking for forgiveness. She is writing a letter to Ralph asking for forgiveness. *It is not because I do not love you. It was all impulse. All impulse. Why did I take the scissors, a gift from John from Switzerland. Why did I take the scissors and on an impulse grab your hand and stab that hand, that hand that had been an instrument of your love? It was an impulse. Yes, an impulse. And after all the wound was slight. Only the blood flowed. But not flowed. No, oozed. I see you running to the bathroom faucet. Pouring peroxide on that wound. I see the white foam. I hear the hissing. I see your pale face. I see the hatred on your face. I am caught in the net of that hatred now. And I now know that hate is as near love as blood is near the surface of the skin. Don't you know that too?*

She has written it all down. She has put down matter-of-factly that she was ready to kill. That her intentions were murderous. She was not pouting, not being coy or merely uncivil. She had made a gesture of murder. She had been violent. Impulsive, unrestrained,

129

irrational. And unmotivated. What had Ralph done? He had been sitting next to her, holding his wineglass in one hand and her own hand in the other. He had dropped her hand in order to light a cigarette. Had squeezed it ever so gently before making the move toward the lighter. In that instant, she had grabbed the scissors lying so casually on the cocktail table (how inelegant could she be, a scissors on her table before the arrival of Ralph? A murderous intent, a premeditated act?). She had grabbed the scissors and had quickly taken his hand, turned it over so that the palm was available, available for that dagger thrust. Her movements were so quick Ralph was absolutely stunned as he watched not her but the red wine oozing onto the couch. She was so quick she too was stunned as she watched the blood ooze. In a moment she had become an expert in violence: she had the speed, the maneuverability, the weapon. She had it all there before the act. After such knowledge, what forgiveness? She could not forgive herself. The knowledge was the act. The act followed the impulse. The cause of the impulse remained even now unknown.

It was John she hated, not Ralph. It was John she wished to hurt. Manipulation of memory, reversal of intent. Substitution of lovers. Sublimation of feeling. Responsiveness to stimulus. Responsiveness to past hurt. Activity processed out of mind, no, out of hand through feeling. What gut told what story of what passion. What passion led to what sequence of events. Event is hard fact. The process of it, that is, the sequence of feelings toward the fact, still unknown. Better unknown. She would not try to probe for reasons. The irrational is superior to the rational. Instinct is authenticity. Reason is manipulative; therefore, not authentic. She is looking for authenticity. In act, in heart. She sits at her desk, puts down her pen. She looks out of the window. At the broken fence covering the hydrangea bush, damaging the hydrangea bush. The fence is made of old wood, of the birch tree the hurricane had toppled, the birch that had been shaped into thin poles flattened and then rounded at the ends. She watches a squirrel run up and down the poles. Another smaller squirrel follows. They are playing some kind of tag. They leave the fence and run up the bare-limbed branches of the dogwood tree. How quickly they scramble from branch to branch. Lithe creatures. Not loathing. Playing. They negotiate each branch as if it were as thick and wide as a tiled roof. Without fear. Dexterity. Unconcern with the spaces all around them. If one should fall, what would the other do? Run away? Come to its aid, drag it to a squirrel home? Under, in what tree do these particular squirrels live? Are these squirrels *chez moi?* How do I give them stability, sanctity, the right not to be considered trespassers?

She turns away from the window. Goes down to the living room. Opens the drawer of the antique desk that John had given her only two years ago for her birthday and takes out the scissors. She had cleaned it thoroughly. Not a trace of blood. Who could tell what treacherous act it had committed? Could detectives discover her beastiality? But Ralph would keep it all to himself out of shame. So slight a matter, only a matter between the two of them. A matter that separated skin from blood vessel, that separated Ann Beaton from Ralph Lenz. A simple matter after all. It told only the story of her life, but even as it told it it concealed it. The act had been direct, immediate, without digression. The reason for it still smothered in blood vessels that were where—in the head or the heart or the arms? Who had asked her recently where she considered her unconscious to be? Oh yes, a poet. He did not like her answer: that it was everywhere. He thought another poet had a much more suggestive response: in the throat, he had said. In the throat. Was that really so preposterous a reply as she had thought at the time? Or was hers, that it was everywhere, a more ridiculous retort. She knew she had said that out of total repression because she really thought her unconscious was in her head. Where she considered all memory, all thought lay. Was she not right? The unconscious even as it gathered up the instinctual, the irrational, the archetypal, certainly could not gather itself into some kind of laryngeal refuge. *But she has glottal stop.* Oh no. Punning won't relieve her, won't solve the problem of her violence. Is she then, has she always been, potentially violent? One action is never complete in itself. It must go backward and forward. Out of the deep past into a present, and protruding into a future. Of course she could go to her old analyst. But he never had helped her. And how does she know that help is what she now needs? Maybe it is not Ralph, not John, but all men. Maybe this is the result of her sympathy for the woman's movement. It led to spontaneous eruptions of overt acts of hostility toward men, any man, lover, husband, friend. And though Ralph was a lover whom she trembled, ached in her love to be with, she obviously felt him a proper target of woman's cumulative hate. She had thrust her manicuring scissors into his palm. She had committed an act of hate toward a man she thought she loved. And what did he do? Run to the faucet, clean the wound, pour over it peroxide, place a Band-Aid on the now dry cut, stride out of bathroom, hall, living room, walk to the closet, take one look at her through the hall mirror, gaze for a moment at his own pale face, adjust the Band-Aid, open the door, walk out. She had never said a single word. Nor had he. After two years, he had simply walked out of her door. After two years, she had simply cut the hand that fed her her existence, her hope, her heart. For two years he had made existence possible, even a future possible, as it had been with John before their divorce. Time was no longer dreary. She had found that her one single self could multiply, not through a child. She had never wanted children—but through her lover. One and another. A lover made two in one. Such arithmetic was begotten out of tenderness. Recently invitations always ended with, "And do invite handsome Ralph." The simplicity of the thing, before. Now silence. Now guilt. Not a guilt of deception as their first year of love had been before her divorce but a guilt of murderous intent. Of a horrendous deed committed, not even long premeditated. A deed spontaneous and terrible. She holds the scissors in her hand as if it were a talisman, a tender offering from a god, a gift from a beloved (as indeed it had been). Yes, it is a gift from a beloved. It showed her the complexity of her love. It showed her that a love thrust could be as dire as rape. The love act, it told her, was not a simple motion growing out of a growing fever, a yearning for physical release. The love act could tear the flesh, pierce even an open palm. She looks yearningly at the scissors. Tears fall from her eyes. This little weapon, this cosmetic aid, she had propelled into her lover's palm. It was then an instrument of love! And yes an instrument of hate. Therefore, it held in itself a complex of emotions, a true love since love was so complex, since love contained the ambiguity of hate and love, since its duplicity was not a duplicity of evil, but a container of the double vision of love itself: the love that looked inward and saw in the love act the symbol of those tensions within it, that simple ambiguity of love: the motions of love that propelled relief and joy also moved in a manner of force, of powerful thrust so that pain could be its accompaniment. Was not that frictional thrust a thrust of hate as well as of love? Was that not the physical embodiment, the dialectic of love? Her act of violence was thus a symbolic act of a love. The pain she inflicted was her love. It was an erotic maneuver. It was physical love.

She walks over to the window holding the scissors in her right hand. The sun is casting shadows, shadows of trees on the roof of the house opposite to her. The shadows are absolutely motionless. She holds up the scissors toward the sun. The points gleam. Sparkle. She moves the prongs nearer to the window. They glint and seem to make her hand warm. She makes small circles with the scissors on the cold window. Now the glint is in her eyes. She feels its penetration. That glint is not circumspect. Not hidden. It is making her smile. She opens her mouth and begins to hum. It is Beethoven's "Ode to Joy." Over and over again she hums the initial phrase, never able to reach the final tonic note. She hums, and hums. Suddenly she stops. The room is filled with her laughter. She laughs and laughs and laughs. The scissors falls out of her hand. Tears begin to flow. She cannot stop those tears. Her whole body is crying. She is on the floor. *I am guilty,* she is whispering between the sobs. An hour passes. She lies quietly, still on the floor. Her eyes open. She hears herself saying over and over, *I am guilty. I am guilty.* She is frowning, frowning. She is puzzled. *Of what am I guilty?* she asks.

FIVE POEMS

ANDREA MOORHEAD

BLACK AMBER

it is only ten after four and the whole sky
is filled in light, filled and to this filling rose black amber,
and i can feel the entire weight of the globe,
ease
and on me too this light raining down,
this slit at dusk, where the pines are freed,
and the long silence between clouds,
so gold, and the rose upon us as rose at dawn,
and the palest moon shape,
as in the early morning,
to my mind, my eyes, my skin,
it is only ten after four, and the whole day
is filled in stars, the whole day is aching
with light and this somber flat shield
of air.

OF APPLE BOUGH AT NIGHT

rain the night so cold i can feel no fever,
or mint stirring above soil,

where print of hands and the sharp rise of foot on stone,
above a garden lit in cherry and blossoming judas,
where a wreathing lemon light and this strange silence
between the hours
fills my heart in a heavy mindless stone,
fills where i wash and cleanse,
where i pull in the night veil, singing in a voice beyond
wind, where the night rains down slowly, and my lost few
hours crack upon me, pulling the richness low to the earth,
pulling this light into blood and heart, where i can not
capture essence or scent, the wild cloy fragrance
of apple bough
at night.

VISAGE AFTER DEATH

For Léo

there's a new vein in the hill,
a black golden rod
blooming crimson
and the violet air
turns my hide yellow and golden,
as sleep begins
to find summer
eased and a long cool breath
trembling
in my hands.

ODE TO LÉO

visage of night
which trembles

as i hold
in my hands
warm fur
and black soiling the root
violet and pure, as a face
evades sun
and the wan moon is cherishing
snow and sharp
raining
the wet soil
forgives
which my hands blunder
and seek
to restore.

PRINT OF SNOW

wherever you have fallen is print of snow,
a crust sparkling and new, where frost blues and the rain
softens, where dew into light entering as veil
and light onto my hands as the aching of soil and rain too
has a light into this speed.
wherever i have fallen is sound of water,
and the salt crystals leave trace too,
under the leaves and bark,
under the floating, diminished
lights.

wherever you have spoken
is a drop of light,
a bead of honey
where the rain cannot sink,
and a rose petal emerges as the sight of day.

wherever i have spoken
a wind so cool

and the black air entering fills my lungs,
to whiten the rage,
cool down the thirst,
tend these fevers
deep in bone and gut.

whenever the rain over us, and fever melting all this snow,
has begun without trace or vapor, has begun deep in evening
when the coolness descends, and a long window of air
to my eyes appearing is new.

there is a veil of night vision, a veil so dense and pure,
my hands waver at sight, and my lips to drink
do obeisance.

OCCAM'S ELECTRIC RAZOR

RUSSELL HALEY

It was a dud. Holliday stood in front of the mirror being given back to himself blanched, skin erupting with bristles, a breath reverberating off the glass. Except for the razor not working he was in a lovely frame of mind. It was his mind which set him apart, other, from the razor.

The latter was an old device, perhaps the earliest model, in maroon Bakelite. It had belonged to his father and had been deeded to him together with the coverless books on botany, the foreign coins, the carpet slippers which could walk by themselves, an unpaid telephone bill dating back twenty years.

Where there's a will there's a way—he hummed. The razor fizzed. Today was a holiday. He thought about that—could not make anything funny of it—had had the name and all the possible jokes for forty years. Time enough now to take the thing apart and find out why it was a dud.

The metal mesh through which the beard hairs were supposed to thrust was clagged and clogged with ancient detritus of skin and hair. So, presumably, the blade could not wag.

Unplug before doing anything electrical. He yanked the three-pin from the socket, forgetting to switch off first. Holliday saw minute blue flames dart out and back.

There was a screwdriver in the sewing machine, and swiftly he removed the head of the razor. Too late he spread newspaper on the table top. A shower, the looser hair, was lost, would float in air or fall in the silence of the room toward the carpet. He was allergic to house-mites—might even be bustling with antibodies now

138

to his father's ground-up hair. Holliday held himself in check—one sneeze might dissipate the lot.

He tapped the body of the machine down on the *Evening Post*. The debris came out easily and then the serrated blade.

It was all so simple. A small electric motor in the palmgrip converted rotary action to a mechanical, side-to-side vibration through a drive shaft. That shaft slotted in a groove on the underside of the blade. And that in turn slid backward and forward and chopped off the hairs as they prodded through the mesh. Clean, clear the mesh, a spot of Singer oil, and reassemble.

Yet it was his father's reddish hair which was heaped before him, and it had been used so long without being cleaned that he had strata of the archaeology of that face, for the main part of the hair had not fallen out in individual millimetre logs but had come out in a clot. The bonding agent was no doubt the oil from the sebaceous glands of that dissolving face.

So this little lump was a record of that aging which had taken place so swiftly—from red beard through to white in one uneasy month.

Should he bury it? Catch the bus to town and then out again from the central bus station to the suburban home of rest where the healthy ashes were carefully potted underground.

Holliday was swept by a nasty vision of an unseemly game of golf where the lids of the urns were unsealed once a year and final remnants like this in front of him were driven, chipped, and putted down into the hole in which one became all and nothing.

No. He would not go. Today was his holiday. Time to reflect at ease—to move through the house making cups of tea and coffee at unordained times. To eat from tins if he wished and then at night to fall asleep with his mind clenched so tightly that he would think all night in his sleep and so prolong the moment when he had to rise, put on his socks, and then out in a raw autumn to his hated job as an audit clerk. The only ray of light there was a promise of an outside job—checking the accounts, the petty cash, of a branch library. Would the librarian tremble as he moved in through the door?

Ah dear! There must be, there must be something else he could do. But for now—fetch the Silvo, the matches, some cotton wool, and a cloth.

Holliday spent a little while making cotton buds on the empty ends of the matches. One small pull of cotton—a twirl of the little stick and the product could almost be sold it had such a perfect shape. Another, then another. Later he could pull away the soiled cotton wool and still use the matches. Perfect.

He opened the metal polish and wondered briefly whether he should use the paste of extruded and drying stuff which had gathered around the cap. But he decided it would be better to employ the ammonia-scented fluid. He tipped a rounded drop, admired the color and odor, and dipped with his match.

The metal came up bright. In those days they must have used real materials and not the modern botch-metal of melted toothpaste tubes and glue. It shone. The chromium plating had a depth— a midnight blue. When he peered inside this little rectangular trough with the assertive shaft sitting in the middle like a small man in a boat he could see portions of his own face. If he moved this way the shaft appeared to spring from his eye—if that it grew between two isolated teeth.

How would it look if he replugged without the blade or guard and switched to "on"?

What an exciting day it was turning out to be. And to think that he'd been poised to throw this razor out together with the slippers and the coins. Back in the socket—switch on at the wall—he positioned himself again so that he could see his nose in the lake of chrome and oh so gently thumbed the razor switch. The machine sang in his hand. Released from the drag of blade and hair the shaft enjoyed its purest oscillation. It moved so quickly that it hardly even made a blur. His nose (he noticed a blackhead) was scarcely marred. There was merely the faintest suggestion of smoke, but intangible, invisible, edging the white flesh with gun-metal aura.

Holliday had discovered invisibility. He knew the principle of the motion picture but had never imagined that if the frames were driven so fast, as quickly as this, that the characters would disappear in blue, nonodorous haze.

If a clock, for example—yes, it would need to be electric—were driven like this, would the hands appear to cease to move? Would time stand still? And at what o'clock would they seem to jam and lodge?

Click. Slow. Sigh. The dying of vibration. An itch in the palm of the hand. And that meant money in any folklore—just like the crossing of a small black spider.

Forget the tea and coffee. On the strength of this discovery he would have a proper drink. The real bottle—the Christmas gift for "foreigners" he did for a small firm whose accounts were decidedly bent. So. Whisky. Under the sink by the bootblack brushes and the defunct Zebo now that he had an electric range was the bottle of Tomatin five-year-old malt: fine gold lettering and a lovely oval picture in flesh tones of sheds, a railway line, a smoking chimney, and the hills of Inverness Shire where the purest English was spoken and the finest Scotch malt made. But the line and sleepers came toward him, went nowhere really, petered out in the foreground. Did the loaded trains move out so fast that *they* dissolved in air?

Ah! Holliday poured at ease. Now he had several questions to ask himself the day became more tangible and real. The clock, the motion picture, and the train. Lovely problems and no anxiety.

He might just wear the slippers and light the ancient toothmarked pipe. The cool rim of the glass against his lip. The hot liquid. He joked. The first glass went down so fast Holliday did not drink it. No way for malt to go—unlike a train, a clock, a motion picture of John Wayne. The second drink hummed and fumed behind his eyes.

No cuts from this razor. He fondled it. He could be sleek.

He saw himself in his wide, open office. The high and pitched oak desks and awkward stools. And the view from the window of the Civic Centre to the Nurses' Home of the Infirmary. The sketchily opaque windows of the bathrooms. Bosoms, busts, buttocks, bums. Himself sleek as a snake. Smooth, pomaded, wearing another suit and not the drab navy. His mind, moving across the gap, the traffic, with the speed of light, invisible, invading, slowing and emerging.

"My name is Holliday and friends as always in this part of the universe called me Okker until a clever temporary clerk from the university up the hill renamed me Occam!"

He tittered. The Chief Clerk's joke. Three women surprised in the nude—young, middle-aged, old. What do they do? Not scream. Got it? No? The young one covers her you know what, the middle one covers her tits, and the old one claps her hands over her face! Ho, Ho, Arghhh! Get it?

His mind is there in the steam and the soap.

"My name is Holliday."

Neither this nor that nor the other. She soaps with a fat sponge. The pages of his audit book spring open and turn unacknowledged. His face like a moon is lost in bliss.

My love, my lovely wet love, you really should give old Occam a kiss.

Then what? He peels his shirt in his own house. Hair running from belt to throat. A dance to the bedroom and in the double mirrors he sees his back. Hair from the shoulders down. Worn patches on the blades but there and there and there! The rest is just as foul as his trousers slide. Dense thickets between the arse; from the front the diamond running up from it to his chest. The legs—smooth patch only on the calves. Hair all over, springing, curling back and penetrating the skin. Even on *that*. Lift up and bend the head. Like a policeman wearing a fur coat. Or a pig with bristles except for his snout.

"My name is Hairy."

"I can see that."

"Could you love me like this?" Impossible. Like a hair plate and a raw steak.

Holliday snapped back like elastic. Three glasses down and two sheets to the wind.

So he takes up his father's razor. The Bakelite is quite worn where the elder's fingers gripped. Should he open up this plastic case? What do you call these screws with a cross in the head? He has nothing to make them turn. Better to leave well alone. It works.

But as an experiment it would be better to test—subject the thing to ultimate stress. Certainly you would not want to get halfway there and then find yourself with an inanimate object in your hand.

The slippers! Oh yes. He hated them anyway and could not understand why he had not thrown them out unless it was that they retained more of his actual father than those buried dry and cleanly ashes.

So high they could walk. They were greasy inside. More than ten years of bare and unwashed feet had tromped the furry inserts flat. But the outsides still retained some nap—the cartography of moths and use.

Holliday placed them on the table in spite of all superstition about footwear being raised above a certain level. Then the reassembly job. Click. Into your groove you little man and mesh to go over your serrated head.

"Oh." It buzzed gently and with promise.

Holliday began at the heel of a slipper and worked round to the front. The skin beneath the hair was black. The edge of the slipper bent round the shape of the ankle bone. There was the rise of arthritic metatarsal—here he glided round the big balled joint of largest toe.

When Holliday finished he had the black relief skin of his father's feet standing, slightly splayed, on the *Evening Post*. He'd had to empty the razor nine times. The hair of whatever creature they had been was mingled with the red and gray of his father's face. And they stood there like something pure. So pure they almost disappeared.

He needed to pee. The back door with its iron catch felt greasy. The yard with cinder shed and midden was gray. Whitewash flaked off the lavatory walls. The water in the bowl was bland, then rippled, then smudged, and finally a curious green.

Holliday stood, balancing, swaying, feet splayed, knees springing back and locking and then surging forward, the whole thing like the dance of a snake to an inaudible tune, and he saw hair again. Long ones that jutted all of their own. White ones which tried to hide beneath the brown. Ones with a totally exaggerated curl and twist like plants growing in a permanent eclipse.

He took hold of one and pulled. It strained and stretched and straightened and gave. Holliday lifted it to face level. It was like something live. A fatty white creature growing a wiry tail. On impulse he severed the root with his teeth. It was like dough, it was like lard, it was like suet.

If you were starving—could you make a meal of your hair—then nails—then calluses—shifting reluctantly to toe, the lesser ones, then finger joint and arm? Finally the delicacy of tongue when all the limbs had gone?

Oh out of this place! Those were not the questions to people sleep and fill the nights—they would bring him back to day and the tea break sans cigarette and the ledger cracking its spine and the figures which would never cast out quite the same in two adds running and home to the deeded house and the coins so light they could float on undisturbed water.

He went back.

His father was sitting in the chair. All the hair from the *Evening Post* was glued around his chin. His feet were black, and they shone like polished stone.

Holliday gaped and yawned.

"Nay lad," his father said, "I was never laid out proper—close shave, limb break, and coins in the eyes. Not forgetting the arse which lets go its hold."

Holliday summoned a joke.

"But you were burned you old faggot—curled and burned and turned into ash."

"Close shaved, limb break, and pennies for eyes. I wanted it so and lacked it lad."

What time was it? The clock had stopped. The fingers of its hands were spread right over its face. Old woman.

Holliday began to jog on the spot. He rode, he rowed his limbs like a small man in a boat. He was a razor scything through grass. He was a slipper, and he fell down twice.

He would be new. He would be nude. Holliday's clothing fell aside. Newborn with no caul. His mind could shoot into any home with the speed of light but for the drag of hair.

"I'm dreaming of a follicle—I'm dreaming of my son," his father said and faded.

Adam and Eve and Nipmewell went down to the sea to bathe. They were all completely nude and Adam and Eve were drowned. Who do you think was saved?

Nipmewell in a hair shirt. He felt the pinch. There was no fire in the grate. He had no meal inside him. Everything that he could possibly eat was growing from him. This was a holiday, a feast day. Make no bones about that.

Holliday picked up the worn Bakelite thing. His thumb made it go.

He emerged once in the nurses' home with his head shaved. The skin of his scalp was a blue haze.

He tried to talk to them through the fog but they asked what was special about him and his blue head. Their pubic patches gleamed with shampoo and with glue.

He lifted his arm and peed against a tree.

Next at the neck the razor plunged its course. Things would have been simple with Occam's honed and hand-ground razor, but this one merely cut a swathe and not his life. Curlicue dross and follicle growth on this Holliday holiday.

Next were those areas almost unknown even to himself—bum which he rarely saw and dark which he tended to look down on. To facilitate everything he had to remove the mirrors from tallboy and bathroom—both large ones giving a full-length view. He placed them six feet apart. One propped against his father's chair and the other lodged against the table.

At first he did not step inside the light machine. For his father had reappeared. Seen obliquely in one only of the mirrors.

"Where do we go from here?"

"All the way out into silver and then back. As fast as anything in this world can go except for me."

Holliday stepped between the silver sheets. At first the light was slowed by the drag of the remaining but multitudinous hair. He came back at himself so many times. He felt his breath. Holliday moved, and they all moved with him. He put the razor on, and an infinite line of diminishing Hollidays put it on. It buzzed in their hands like something live. No way forward except on, just as his father had said.

His mind popped out to the faintly opaque windows of the nurses' home and one by one, starting at infinity, the little Hollidays slid off and out into the silver and blue haze of damp bathrooms.

All the razors came down between those diminishing buttocks. Hair fell apart in a swirl of smoke.

Nude, hairless except for the very last one, Holliday contemplated the single image which was not reproduced in the mirror behind.

This single and indivisible Occam plied the tenuous and fading maroon machine. He buzzed it down slowly over reaped flesh and began at the very tip of the hair, feeding it in slowly through the mesh. As it reached ground zero, Holliday gave himself one last smile. His breath only started to come back at him but then remained suspended in the room between the sheets of glass which reflected nothing but their own bland and empty surfaces.

Holliday had reached the speed of light.

House, slippers, coins and backless books all waited but the razor had gone—slipped off the edge of everything in a maroon shift with its master. The simplest solution of all.

A PAPER STORY

JULIA OLDER

SUCCESS

Paper boy blew along the street.
"You will have much success,"
I said with clairvoyant eyes
while he read the word
printed across his chest.
"No, he will burn," the others said.
They did not want to let him.
He sat at an outdoor café
with the rain whipping into his face
which soon became thick and soggy.
He had one friend in all the world, a girl.
She lived as much unlike him.
When he could no longer look down
at his frayed corners she replaced the edges
with her delicate fingers.
Sometimes she cut herself
turning him over and over.
But these were minor wounds
compared to the ignominy
they wrote on his soul.

A LAW

Paper boy walked in the sun
and was nearly dry but very yellow
when he stopped in front of the girl's house.
He knew she could use him for something.
There were mornings he awoke perfectly blank.
She wrote on him until he was covered,
even turning him inside out
to do the other side,
(she was a very thorough girl).
They did not like her dedication.
Real girls did not associate with paper boys.
It was a law.
In fact, another paper boy wrote it down himself
after a vision.
Paper boy looked up at her house.
He had a feeling that one day it too
would turn to paper.
Everything he touched seemed to turn.
For fear of this he did not touch her.
What would a paper boy say to a paper girl?
A strong wind sucked him against the gate.
He held his breath so the spikes
would not spear his side.
They walked by conversing loudly and happily.
The sun, after all, had come out.
They remembered having saved him
in some way, and smiled satisfied smiles.
The girl stood in the upstair window
brushing, brushing her hair, hair.

ACCEPTANCE

In his paper mind
paper boy tried

to smell the fragrance of her,
a flower, not of crepe paper
but of velvet petals
pulsing in the breeze.
They accepted her odor,
the color of her skin, her eyes—
true eyes, deep, silent.
She looked down on him.
He felt the lines
appear on his temples,
the lines and margins.
He could not escape them
and so
he followed them
up the sidewalk
to the doormat.
WELCOME,
and so
he went in.

THE MISTAKE

Her mother was in the master bedroom
mastering a hairdryer.
Her father had very little hair.
What he had he parted down the middle.
Why didn't she come down to meet him?
He desperately needed a few more sheets,
her cool fingers on his brittle back,
the caress of her hair
brushed into electricity
so that it leapt like a magnet
to his paper body.
She finished the final stroke and turned
Paper boy
She finished the final stroke and turned

Paper boy stood
She finished
She turned
His alphabetical past was deleted
with that turning, at best cast down,
erased fast, gravely he incorporated
joyous, kind, large memories.
Now opened, paper boy
quivered, ran, stood still.
Time uncovered vast wastepaper.
XYZ slipped by
on the crumbled gum.
"Hello," she said.
A word appeared over the erasure.
He could not stop it from growing.
She brushed him off
and scrutinized the surface.
Paper boy read the word
in the mirror of her eyes.
"You have made a mistake," she whispered.
Tears surrounded the word.
The word swam, but slowly sank
into her violet iris.
Paper boy was relieved.
She knew!
They clamored beneath her window.
"Throw him away.
It's not true. He's worse
than all the paper boys.
Incinerate him."
Paper boy savored
the salt of her tears.
And she savored
the penalty.

INTRUSION

Family dog trotted to the girl
carrying a letter in his canines.
She scooped him to her bosom
which he licked like his bowl.
Paper boy, forgotten,
concentrated on the previous joy.
"Mother, mother!"
He started at this sudden intrusion.
Not only had the girl forgotten him
but in a moment of impatience
her elbow pierced his side,
and then one by one her long fingernails
tapped furiously on his chest.
Mother came running, frizzy and intuitive.
"There's going to be a wedding?
Now you must give me time
to order the invitations.
The reception will be here, of course."
Paper boy smiled in italics.
Well, if she wanted marriage . . .
The others bothered him.
She would be ostracized.
Her mother and father, family dog
would be ostracized.
Why did she keep
folding up his corners
and rolling them down
between her thumb and index?
He voided with pain.
"Oh mother," she said
finally taking her arm from paper boy
who by now was disconsolate
with her carelessness.
"He has asked me to marry him!"
She held up the letter
and then slapped it down
on top of paper boy.

He suffocated in the fine print.
Mother hugged
daughter, hugged
family dog
and paper boy pretended
he wasn't anywhere.
And he wasn't.
Once, she had seen the word
and accepted it.
Now, what served as his paperweight
mattered more to her.
Again she picked up the letter.
Then she saw paper boy
and with a tiny exclamation
picked him up and waved him in the air.
Below they hissed and jeered.
"I guess I won't be needing this anymore."
She held him to the light
and reread every word but one,
the one that would have saved him.

THE END

Real girl walked to the window,
crushing paper boy slowly
in her delicate fingers.
He was a crumpled paper ball
when she threw him down
to their outstretched hands.

KUDAN

UCHIDA HYAKKEN

Translated from the Japanese by Nancy Beckman

Translator's note. *Uchida Hyakken, whose real name was Uchida Eizō, was born in 1889, the only son of an Okayama sake-maker. He began writing in high school, where he studied haiku and started a group that published a student literary magazine. At this time, he took the pen name Hyakken (one hundred ken, or about two hundred yards) from the width of a certain dry river in Okayama. Later, he used a playful variation, Hyakkien ("Garden of One Hundred Ogres").*

In 1909, he sent his short story "Rōneko monogatari" ("The Tale of the Old Cat") to the novelist Natsume Sōseki (1867–1916) and received an encouraging reply. Two years later, while a student at Tokyo Imperial University, he met Sōseki and joined his group of disciples. Traces of Sōseki's influence appear in many of Hyakken's works.

Majoring in German literature, Hyakken was graduated in 1914 and taught German for the next twenty years. He was professor of German at Hōsei University from 1920 on, but often held simultaneous positions at other institutions as well.

Nineteen-twenty was also an important year for him musically. A koto student from childhood, he was inspired by Miyagi Michio's (1884–1956) performances and began to study with him that year. The two maintained a close relationship until Miyagi's death in 1956. Hyakken's musical life provided the subject matter for many of his writings, most notably "Isobe no matsu" ("The Pine Tree of Isobe"), which is based on Miyagi and the sōkyoku piece "Zangetsu."

The following year, 1921, Hyakken's first collection of short stories, Shinshōsetsu ("New Stories"), was published. It includes "Meido" ("Hades"), "Hanabi" ("Fireworks"), and "Kudan." Nineteen-thirty-three saw the publication of Hyakkien zuihitsu ("Hyakkien's Essays"), which brought him fame as an essayist. In 1934, at the age of forty-five, he resigned from Hōsei to devote more time to his writing. For several years he also worked part-time, until the proceeds from his writing sufficed to support his family.

None of his works have appeared in English translation, but one which may be of interest to Western readers is a parody of Sōseki's I Am a Cat *("Wagahai wa neko de aru," tr. 1961 and 1972), entitled* Gansaku wagahai wa neko de aru *(1950). Hyakken died in 1971.*

"Kudan" was written in 1919. The Chinese character for "kudan" is composed of the elements for "man" 人 *and "bull"* 牛

The dull moon, swollen and yellow, hung in the sky. Behind me, a pale light floated above the horizon, but I couldn't tell whether it was the sunset or the sunrise. A dragonfly glided in front of the yellow moon. When its black silhouette against the moon disappeared, the dragonfly vanished from my sight.

I was standing in the middle of a huge field that stretched as far as I could see. My body was sopping wet, drops fell from the tip of my tail. I had heard of kudans as a child, but never dreamed I would become one. There I was, born a wretched monster with a bull's body and a human face. I stood vacantly in the large, unlit field, wondering what I should do. I had no idea why I had been put there or where the cow that gave birth to me had gone.

Presently the moon turned white. The glow in the sky behind me had faded; in front of me, only a band of light remained above the horizon. The band slowly narrowed until it was on the verge of disappearing, when a great number of small black dots rose in the midst of it. Their number grew rapidly until they filled the horizon, obliterating the light. The sky was dark. Then the moon began to shine. I realized that it was evening, and that the band of light I had seen had been in the western sky. My body gradually dried, and I felt the short hairs on my back quiver each time the wind blew.

The moon shrank, and a pale light flowed far and wide. The field looked as though it were under water. Feelings of regret arose in me as I thought back to my days as a human being. But my memory of the last few days was unclear, and I wasn't sure exactly when my human life had ended. Try as I might, I was unable to recall any details. I bent my forelegs and had a try at lying down, but the sand stuck to my hairless chin, and so I stood up again. I passed the time, now wandering in circles, now standing absently, and the night deepened.

The moon sank in the west, and as dawn approached, a wind came from the west like a great wave. Sniffing the sand brought by the wind, I mused, "This will be my first day as a kudan." Suddenly a terrifying thought came to me: I had forgotten that a kudan dies three days after its birth. Moreover, it prophesies good or evil for the future. Having been born such a miserable creature, I didn't mind dying so soon, but I was worried about making a prophecy. First of all, I couldn't imagine what I would predict. How fortunate I was to be in the middle of a field with no one around to expect a prophecy. I could die alone without having to say anything.

Just then the wind from the west brought loud voices. Surprised, I looked in that direction, and again the wind blew. This time I heard a voice saying, "Over there, over there." I had heard the voice somewhere before.

Then I realized that the black dots which had appeared on the horizon the day before had been people. They had spent all night crossing the field to hear my prophecy. What a predicament! There was nothing to do but escape before they caught me, and so I galloped as fast as I could to the east. The pale light streaming in the eastern sky rapidly turned white, revealing a frightful swarm of people moving toward me like the shadow of a black cloud. The wind shifted and blew from the east, carrying excited shouts. "Over there, over there," I heard as clearly as if it came from beside me. This, too, was a familiar voice. Startled, I dashed to the north, whereupon a north wind began to blow. A huge crowd rushed toward me riding on the wind and shouting, "Over there, over there." When I tried the south, the wind shifted again. Hordes of people were closing in on me from all sides. There was no escape.

Multitudes were coming to hear me utter a prophecy. I could imagine how enraged they would be when they found out that this kudan wasn't going to predict anything. I didn't mind dying on the third day, but I cringed at the thought of being tormented until then. I stomped my hooves in vexation. The dull moon, swollen and yellow, hung in the western sky. It was the same scene as the previous evening. I stared bewildered at the moon.

Night gave way to dawn.

The people surrounded me at a distance. It was a tremendous crowd—thousands, perhaps tens of thousands. Ten or twenty of them came forward and began to work busily in front of me. They hauled out lumber and built a wide fence around me. Behind it, they constructed platforms supported by scaffolding.

Presently it was midday. Since I had nothing else to do, I gazed at the builders. My guess was that they planned to sit on the platforms and wait for my prediction. Hemmed in by the crowd, I had no idea what to do; after all, I had nothing to predict. I wanted to escape, but there was no way out.

The completed platforms rapidly turned black as they filled with people. When there was no more room, the rest of the people stood under the platforms or squatted near the fence.

Before long, a man in a white robe came out from under the platform to the west and quietly approached me holding a ladle in both hands, like an offering. There was a deathly stillness. He advanced solemnly until he was directly in front of me, then put the ladle on the ground and retraced his steps. It contained sparkling, clear water. Apparently he wanted me to drink the water, and so I did. Suddenly, all around me, the people began to shout.

"Look, he drank it, he drank it!"

"He drank it at last! Pretty soon now!"

I looked around in surprise. They seemed to think that I would make my prediction after I drank the water. But I had nothing to say, and so I turned away and walked around aimlessly. It was already close to sundown. I wished that night would come soon.

"Hey! It turned away!"

"Maybe it won't speak today."

"It's taking so long, no doubt it'll make a momentous prediction."

Recognizing all of these voices, I scanned the crowd. Crouching behind the fence and staring at me was a man I vaguely remembered. I couldn't be sure at first, but the longer I observed him, the more certain I was that I knew him. Then I looked around and saw the faces of my friends, relatives, teachers, and students pressed in a row against the fence. Elbowing one another aside to get a good view, they all stared at me. I felt sick at the sight of them.

"Say, doesn't it look like someone you know?"

"Really? I'm not sure."

"It looks like somebody, but I can't think who."

I was flustered when I heard that. I would have been ashamed for my friends to learn that I was an animal, and so I decided not to turn my face in that direction any more.

While I was unaware of it, the sun had set; the dull yellow moon hung in the sky. The moon slowly turned white, and the platforms and fence dissolved into darkness as night fell. People started bonfires around the fence; flames flowed all night in the moonlit sky. The crowd sleeplessly awaited my prediction. The reddish-grey smoke floating in front of the moon gradually blackened, the light of the moon faded, and a dawn wind blew.

Again night yielded to daybreak. It looked as though thousands more had crossed the field during the night. People were coming and going incessantly outside the fence, rowdier than the day before. They seemed even less likely to settle down, and I became more and more anxious.

Soon, the man in the white robe approached with the ladle again. As before, it held water. He ceremoniously offered it to me and retreated. I knew that if I drank it again the crowd would assume that I was going to say something, and so I didn't even look at it. Besides, I didn't want any water.

"It's not drinking."

"Keep still. You mustn't talk at a time like this."

"I'm sure it has an important prediction. Must be something big if it's taking this long."

Again there was a commotion behind me as people moved impatiently this way and that. The man in white came up to me again and again, presenting the water. The people were silent as he brought it, but each time they saw me refuse to drink, their clamor increased. He set the water closer to me each time, until finally he pushed it directly under my nose. This annoying behavior angered me. Then another man came forward with the ladle. When he had almost reached me, he stopped and glared at me, then strode right up and thrust the ladle in my face. He looked familiar, and though I wasn't sure who he was, he infuriated me. When I refused to drink the water, he clicked his tongue in annoyance.

"Won't you drink?"

"I don't want any," I snapped.

Pandemonium followed. Startled, I looked around to see people jumping from the platforms and others climbing over the fence, shouting as they rushed toward me.

"It spoke!"

"It finally said something!"

"What did it say?"

"No, it's about to speak."

The yellow moon had risen, and daylight was fading. At last the sun would set on the second day. I still had nothing to predict, and yet I didn't feel as though I were about to die. Possibly, I thought, a kudan dies because it makes a prophecy; if I didn't predict anything, perhaps I wouldn't have to die on the third day. Suddenly life was precious. I reasoned that it would be better not to die.

Just then the fastest runner from the crowd reached me. He was immediately pushed out of the way by the person behind him, who, in turn, was shoved aside by the next one. "Calm down, calm down!" they shouted at one another. Terrified of what the disappointed, enraged throng might do if they caught me, I was desperate to escape, but it would have been impossible to break through the solid wall of people. The clamor rose until it was deafening; shrieks filled the air. The human wall was closing in on me. I was paralyzed with fear. In a daze, I took a drink from the ladle. A hush fell over the crowd. Then I came to my senses and realized what I had done, but there was no way to undo it. Seeing the people's expectant faces made me even more fearful. A cold sweat oozed from my entire body. I remained silent; the din began again and gradually increased.

"Wonder why he's not saying anything. Strange, isn't it?"

"He'll speak soon. It's sure to be something startling."

The commotion wasn't as agitated as before, and when I looked closely, the crowd seemed ill at ease. Less afraid, I gazed at the individuals in the front row. I recognized all of them. Their faces were clouded with anxiety and dread. I calmed down. Suddenly thirsty, I took another sip of water. This time no one said anything. The shadow of anxiety darkened; for a time, it seemed as though everyone was holding his breath.

"I'm afraid."

It was a low voice, but it resounded throughout the area. The human wall had expanded; people were backing away from me bit by bit.

"I'm afraid to listen. At this rate, there's no telling what the kudan will say."

"Whether the prophecy is good or bad, it's better not to hear it. Hurry up and kill the kudan before it says anything."

That startled me. I couldn't bear to be killed. And I was certain it was the voice of my own son. The voices I had heard until then had all been familiar, but I couldn't identify them, this one I remember. Hoping to catch a glimpse of my son, I started to get up.

"The kudan raised its forelegs!"

"It's going to make a prophecy!"

At that instant, the human wall, which had surrounded me without a gap, suddenly collapsed. With a frightened surge of energy, the silent crowd jumped over the fence, scrambled under the platforms, and scattered in all directions.

Sunset was drawing near. The yellow moon began to glow dimly. Relieved, I stretched my forelegs. Then I yawned widely three or four times. Somehow I felt that I wasn't going to die.

DEATHMASK OF THE POET

MICHAEL MOTT

In early summer
paperwasps have scraped
our redwood arbor bare
to build a hive
against our windows

From weaving studio
and garden
we see both sides
of everything

The coating
and the core
cling to convenient skin
a different kind of air

Now when she weaves
beyond the uprights
of a loom
also of redwood
but untouched
among wood crosses
in its loose wrappings
some portent stirs

continually
is always
upon the point of being

Each day
indoors
a little larger bundle
grows in our sleep
or inattention
against the glass

Outside the hive
becomes heraldic
gains a crown
of question marks
tire tracks
in bister snow
sea scrolls
owl feathers
grey and brown

Only by certain light
between the shadows
this shape
looks like a head

The open O
emits its Orphic notes
blurred
barred
old gold
to each green corner
of the underworld
our garden

Rilke
today I traced
what Paula saw
and painted

when you both were young
and Clara also
three small uncertain figures
standing beside a Northern sea

People wear out
their possibilities of faces
far too fast
thought Malte
once
your surrogate

But you
held onto this one
Rainer Maria Rilke
made it
the tragi-comic mask
and map
of where you'd been

Yet it declared
declaimed
not one
of all your poems

Only the broken notes
only the years
of sponging on the rich
the loved ones
left behind
so early
first
for things
and beasts
then angels

One Orpheus
who never cried
"Euridice!"

What has
abandoned you
the un-face
mummy cloth
the lining
thin as paper
through all its
breaking places
says
how seldom
the human really works

Tonight
only the shuttles talk
my own face
hangs on glass

Insects like miners
inch through
the inner layers
on belly
or on back
under our lamps

I think of your idea
of running needles
over the grooves
of craniums
to let
the thoughtwaves speak

then watch these insects
roam their labyrinth
by instinct

wondering what California redwoods
and paperwasps
might sing together
or apart

what cry for human cry
crisscrossing poems
play always
out of our range

SLOWLY BUMBLING IN THE VOID

CAROL EMSHWILLER

There is a need in all of us to build a little house, log by log or stone by stone. There is a need to sew up a little mattress for the floor, to stash away dried food in leather pouches (rice and figs), a need to make a little set of shelves and to put up a hook for our coat and another hook for our pan. There is a need to make soup out of old bones, to gather dandelion greens and prepare them according to a grandmother's recipe. Then there is a need that a storm should rage outside and that we should sleep through it. Afterwards, after, that is, the need to make a map of the territory, there is a need in all of us to move in time to some kind of tapping, to move (decorated and with hat) to tunes or to play a game with small stones and, all the while, to be on the lookout for something mysterious.

There is a need in me to knit a scarf for you, to make (for you) an overcoat out of a blanket. There is a need to string a wire from the telephone to the pole in order to call you up. There is a need for a calendar of the coming year in order to write down what will happen in the future and in order to mark an X on the days when you will be here. There is a need for a little alarm clock and perhaps a little wind-up toy that hops and turns in circles with a clicking sound. (These are for you.)

I also want to prepare for you a fish that you caught with your bare hands in my stream. I need to prepare your fish. I need to hear you call me by my name holding out your fish.

"I said I want to cook your fish! Were you listening to me then? Are you listening to me now?"

He isn't listening.

He has a funny shape for a hero, but then I have never been known as a full-breasted woman.

It's still the simple life, except now, to go anywhere, one always needs keys and a watch.

Speak of the hero before he appears (under the black, ceremonial umbrella) saying: These are the beloved's dark brown socks. (Your socks.) Here, his dirty shirt. It is his hairs that are stuck in the comb. This is where he spilled his drink. This is where he put his fist through the wall saying, "We must find a peaceful solution to our marriage." But he has put his cheek against my birthmark. He has licked lint from my navel. He has washed my feet.

But already it's several years later and we have moved on now into a whole other category. You've turned the cottage into a TV station or it might as well be. I'm not the star here even though I'm blinded by lights that are reflected in the surfaces of utensils and mirrors that belong to both of us. My blemishes are revealed and catalogued and held against me. "Oh." I say it for the camera. "Oh, wind, sand and dim (suburban) stars . . . vast plain with here and there a ridiculous promontory . . ." (It's Long Island. New York is on the horizon. Perhaps life would be better here if it were the other way around.)

So how do I look on my way to the waterfall, especially now that it's several years later? Still shrouded in mystery? Still seen as though from behind a scrim of desire? Though how long can a scrim like that last? Look. This is me leaning over to drink from the water. This is me taking off one shoe and putting my foot in even though it's ice cold. This is you, happening to notice my foot. I believe I have revealed another blemish. Wanting to come across and "nice" (at the very least) and, above all, feminine, I describe myself to you as liking the babies of all species. I tell you that I would drop food from my mouth into their little mouths in a moment of need not even necessarily dire. But how begin to describe myself even to myself? How do it when caught suddenly between short hair and long? Between the big middle period of life and old age? Between one kind of love and the next higher form? Another day, in other words, and a whole other category of existence in which I may even make a move in the direction of freedom . . . freedom, that is, around a fixed point. (You.)

But he has turned away already, crying out: "Direct access," (a not unfamiliar cry where the media is concerned) or is it, "Direct success"?

He burped on TV once.
I had to hold my mouth right. I had to hold my breath. I had to try to look *beyond* the lights.

How make love grow? (There is a need.) (There is a responsibility.) Proceed along given lines set forth in certain books. (It's already an exact science.) Don't wait to be asked! Keep both hands busy at the same time. Mouth. He may be grateful. (I kissed his instep.)

In your dream you were proud of your enormous penis. You showed it off to me suspecting I would like it, and you were right, I didn't, even in your dream. In my dream the vagina stuck out like a duck's beak and snapped up everything it could reach. In your dream you puffed yourself up still farther until it would have taken some giantess to engulf you. In my dream it wasn't a question of size, but that the vicious vagina could snap off your hand if you reached for me. In answer to my dream you dreamed your giant penis tore me in two. In my next dream you went limp all of a sudden (probably from some remark of mine) and had to stuff your long, weak self down your left pant leg and on into your shoe.

He wants to take good care of his penis.
He wants to make good use of it.

There is a need in me to make a gesture in the direction of freedom outwards from a fixed point which is you. There is a need to project an upward climb and to make promises (if only to myself) and to make, also, a little chart for the wall in order to keep track of the progress. Freedom is up the left-hand side. Love is marked along the bottom line. No, I mean time, in increments of half a day, along the bottom. Progress is inevitably outwards, therefore, from the fixed point of what we used to be to each other. There may be happy accidents. One can look forward to them. A complete new repertoire of behavior may be possible for both of us, including reversal of roles, dancing, rage, and even mediocrity. (I have sometimes, here on this featureless plain, made myself bland out of the fear of being bland.)

Up to now, we have been leading a kind of once-over-lightly life.

Here on this plain, New York on the horizon, futile rustic gestures in the form of tree-lined streets, you have offered me cookies. These are the cookies of love. (This is in a dream.) I laugh behind my hand and only pretend to be delighted. I don't dare take any and I act out an enthusiasm for them that I do not feel. Why, in this dream, do I not allow myself to take them? Why, in this dream, do I want to laugh at you?

Even so, I give you the run of my little house, but you want more headroom.

Reality appears in the form of a long journey. You have gone to the mountainous region in search of direct access and a hands-on experience though you have professed to be in search of semiprecious stones.

You, yourself, become the missing element.

You are no longer under the ceremonial black umbrella.

I wear a monkey's skull on the other end of my tether. (It's for show. I have tied it there myself.)

A hundred years ago this land was marshland. It's no wonder, then, that all the promontories collapse in the mud, that all roads become impassable, and that I can't even make my way to my own kitchen where I had hoped to conduct experiments (culinary) on your fist. I mean, fish. (It has crawled away gasping. I heard it in the middle of the night.) I will call you up. (Assuming, that is, that I can make it to the phone.) I want to tell you something that's not a defense or a pretense or an explanation.

At this moment I yearn to re-invent the wheel, heating damp wood until it can be forced to form a circle, making a light, quick vehicle for myself. I want to re-invent it slowly, one step at a time, first as a toy, later on in a bicycle, then a VW, skipping the ox cart altogether or anything ponderous. But I hardly get started before you return of your own accord, having tied your fig leaf back on the tree. You are humming. "Come share an intimate moment with me and the camera," you are saying. You order more film and a drum and a flute and a basket of feathers. This reunion is a once-in-a-lifetime opportunity. The possibility of muffing it makes you, or so you tell me, feel as if you are adrift in a small, unseaworthy boat. Perhaps you have, in the hiatus, become a poet of sorts. The children (there actually are children by now) are told not to expect too much from Daddy and Mommy in the next few days. The title of your new work will be: SEE THE LOVERS STILL AT-TACKED. I know you mean, ATTACHED . . . STILL AT-TACHED. You missed it by only one letter.

I see by the chart on our wall that we have moved on up into another category. The tan line, which was followed for a short time by a sort of ugly grayish-green line, is now followed by the beginnings of a more or less blue line. There is an infinitesimal, but clearly perceptible upward swing. We are also one full square outwards. Love is along the top and to be aimed for. Time, at a quarter of an inch for half a day, is along the bottom. Freedom (a subdivision of space) is outwards from a fixed point. (You.)

We hollow out a log in order to see what sort of musical instrument will result. Then we will move, decorated and with hats.

Categories are lies believers tell.

All the other disasters (deaths, for instance) will come later.

TWELVE POEMS

SYLVIA TOWNSEND WARNER

AZRAEL

Who chooses the music, turns the page,
Waters the geraniums on the windowledge?
Who proxies my hand,
Puts on the mourning ring in lieu of the diamond?

Who winds the trudging clock, who tears
Flimsy the empty date off calendars?
Who widow-hoods my senses
Lest they should meet the morning's cheat defenseless?

Who valets me at nightfall, undresses me of another day,
Puts it tidily and finally away,
And lets in darkness
To befriend my eyelids like an illusory caress?

I called him Sorrow when first he came,
But Sorrow is too narrow a name;
And though he has attended me all this long while
Habit will not do. Habit is servile.
He, inaudible, governs my days, impalpable,
Impels my hither and thither. I am his to command,
My times are in his hand.
Once in a dream I called him Azrael.

THREE POEMS

Experimentally poking the enormous
Frame of the universe
This much we know:
It has a pulse like us.

But if it lags for woe,
Quickens for fever
Or calm euphoria measures it for ever
Other astronomers must show.

·

Learning to walk, the child totters between embraces;
Admiring voices confirm its tentative syllables.
In the day of unlearning speech, mislaying balance,
We make our way to the grave delighting nobody.

·

Fish come solid out of the sea,
Each with its due weight of destiny.
The purposed sprat knows what it would be at,
The skate, twirling in its death agony,
Is the embodied wave that flopped down
On the fisherman's coble and left him to drown.

DORSET ENDEARMENTS

"My Doll, my Trumpery!"
O sleepy child lulled on the jogging knee
With eyes brilliant as gems new-fetched from the gloom
Of the mine you stare about the cottage room.

On the ceiling badged with smoke the flies crawl.
The flowery paper sags from the damp wall, .
The wind bellows in the dark chimney throat, the rain
Darkens the dishclout stuffed in the broken pane.

Tick-tock. Tick-tock.
Time drips like water from the alarm clock
That jars your Daddy from bed for the milking at five,
And will do the same for you if you live and thrive.

And before the narrow fire on the wide hearth
She sings to her child, to her jewel new-fetched from the dark
Of the womb, and dandles him on a weary knee:
"My Doll, my Trumpery!"

BALLAD STORY

When I was young
And went to the school,
I saw Kate Dalrymple,
Who was so tall,
Who was so tall,
So laughing and lily-smooth
That I loved her before I knew
What it is to love.

What it is to love
I have studied since then,
But never so deeply
As that midnight when,
With daybreak departing,
I betook me alone
To lie at her doorstep
And kiss the stone,

And kiss it and kiss it,
That dumb doorstone
Where her foot would be set
When I was far and gone.

Then I was gone
To learn to be a man,
To make a fortune
According to plan;
And according to plan
And forty years after
I came back by air
Who had gone by water.

Ebbed and flowed the water
While Kate Dalrymple
Crossed the same doorstone,
Heard the years ripple,
Heard the years trample,
Till at last she was led
Into the hospital
To lie on a high bed,

To lie on a high bed
And look at the wall.

GRAVEYARD IN NORFOLK

Still in the countryside among the lowly
Death is not out of fashion,
Still is the churchyard park and promenade
And a new-made grave a glory.
Still on Sunday afternoons, contentedly and slowly,
Come widows eased of their passion,
Whose children flitting from stone to headstone facade
Spell out accustomed names and the same story.

From mound to mound chirps grasshopper to grasshopper:
John dear husband of Mary,
Ada, relict, Lydia the only child,
Seem taking part in the chatter.
With boom and stumble, with cadence and patient cropper,
The organist practises the voluntary,
Swallows rehearsing their flight sit Indian-filed,
And under the blue sky nothing is the matter.

With spruce asters and September roses
Replenished are jampots and vases,
From the breasts of the dead the dead blossoms are swept
And tossed over into the meadow.
Women wander from grave to grave inspecting the posies,
And so tranquilly time passes
One might believe the scything greybeard slept
In the yew tree's shadow.

Here for those that mourn and are heavy laden
Is pledge of Christ's entertainment;
Here is no Monday rising from warm bed,
No washing or baking or brewing,
No fret for stubborn son or flighty maiden,
No care for food or raiment;
No sweeping or dusting or polishing need the dead,
Nothing but flowers' renewing.

Here can the widow walk and the trembling mother
And hear with the organ blended
The swallows' auguring twitter of a brief flight
To a securer staying;
Can foretaste that heavenly park where toil and pother,
Labour and sorrow ended,
They shall stroll with husband and children in blameless white,
In sunlight, with music playing.

EARL CASSILIS'S LADY

Meeting her on the heath at the day's end,
After the one look and the one sigh, he said,
Did a spine prick you from the goosefeather bed?
Were the rings too heavy on your hand?
Were you unhappy, that you had to go?
No.

Was it the music called you down the stair,
Or the hot ginger that they gave you then?
Was it for pleasure that you followed them
Putting off your slippers at the door
To dance barefoot and blood-foot in the snow?
No.

What then? What glamoured you? No glamour at all;
Only that I remembered I was young
And had to put myself into a song.
How could time bear witness that I was tall,
Silken, and made for love, if I did not so?
I do not know.

DECEMBER 31ST ST SILVESTER

Silvester, an old harmless pope,
Stands at the year's end and gazes outward;
And time his triple crown has shredded
And winters have frayed out his cope.

He is white as the weathered bladebone;
Bleached in the rim of his name like winter honesty
He rattles on the stem of history
And is venerated at Pisa alone.

But green in his hand is a twig of olive;
For in his reigning days he devised a reign

Of peace with the Emperor Constantine;
And he watches the years to see it arrive.

IN APRIL

I am come to the threshold of a spring
Where there will be nothing
To stand between me and the smite
Of the martin's scooping flight,
Between me and the halloo
Of the first cuckoo.
"As you hear the first cuckoo,
So you will be all summer through."
This year I shall hear it naked and alone;
And lengthening days and strengthening sun will show
Me my solitary shadow,
My cypressed shadow—but no,
My Love, I was not alone; in my mind I was talking with you
When I heard the first cuckoo,
And gentle as thistledown his call was blown.

GLORIANA DYING

None shall gainsay me. I will lie on the floor.
Hitherto from horseback, throne, balcony,
I have looked down upon your looking up.
Those sands are run. Now I reverse the glass
And bid henceforth your homage downward, falling
Obedient and unheeded as leaves in autumn
To quilt the wakeful study I must make
Examining my kingdom from below.
How tall my people are! Like a race of trees
They sway, sigh, nod heads, rustle above me,

And their attentive eyes are distant as starshine.
I have still cherished the handsome and well-made:
No queen has better masts within her forests
Growing, nor prouder and more restive minds
Scabbarded in the loyalty of subjects;
No virgin has had better worship than I.
No, no! Leave me alone, woman! I will not
Be put into a bed. Do you suppose
That I who've ridden through all weathers, danced
Under a treasury's weight of jewels, sat
Myself to stone through sermons and addresses,
Shall come to harm by sleeping on a floor?
Not that I sleep. A bed were good enough
If that were in my mind. But I am here
For a deep study and contemplation,
And a Persephone, and the red vixen,
Go underground to sharpen their wits,
I have left my dais to learn a new policy
Through watching of your feet, and as the Indian
Lays all his listening body along the earth
I lie in wait for the reverberation
Of things to come and dangers threatening.
Is that the Bishop praying? Let him pray on.
If his knees tire his faith can cushion them.
How the poor man grieves Heaven with news of me!
Deposuit superbos. But no hand
Other than my own has put me down—
Not feebleness enforced on brain or limb,
Not fear, misgiving, fantasy, age, palsy,
Has felled me. I lie here by my own will,
And by the curiosity of a queen
I dare say there is not in all England
One who lies closer to the ground than I.
Not the traitor in the condemned hold
Whose few straws edge away from under his weight
Of ironed fatality; not the shepherd
Huddled for cold under the hawthorn bush,
Nor the long, dreaming country lad who lies
Scorching his book before the dying brand.

A JOURNEY BY NIGHT

"In this last evening of our light, what do you carry,
Dark-coloured angels, to the cemetery?"
"It is the Cross we bury.

"Now therefore while the last dews fall,
The birds lay by their song and the air grows chill
Follow us to the burial.

"It was at this hour that God walked discouraged
Seeing his olive grove with a new knowledge
While man hid from his visage;

"It was at this hour the dove returned;
It was at this hour the holy women mourned
Over the body in clean linen wound.

"So God in man lay down, and man at long
Last in the sepulchre was reclining
And the dove laid her head under her wing;

"Only the poor Cross was left standing.

"Scarecrow of the reaped world, it remained uncarried and unwon;
With no companion
But its warping shadow it endured on,

"Till in this final dusk even that shadow,
Stealthy and slow, stealthy and slow
Faded and withdrew.

"So was the last desolation accomplished
And the Cross gave up the ghost.
Look on it now, look your last;

"See how harmless it lies, now it is down;
A shape of timber which in a tree began
And not much taller than the height of a man."

It lay there, naked on the bier. It was black
With tears, blood, martyrdoms, with jewels decked,
And rubbed smooth with wearing on a child's neck.

Shouldering their burden, the angels went onward,
Like a wreath of mist moving unhindered,
And like a mourner I followed.

Time was no barrier to us, for time was no more;
The tideless sea lay muted along the shore,
The city clocks registered no hour,

The last echo had ebbed from the church bells;
Silent were the barracks, silent the brothels
And the water slept in the wells.

Rivers we forded and mountain ranges crossed;
Silent were the reeds in the marshes we traversed;
Silent as they we came to a coast

And smelled the sea beneath us and walked dry-footed
On air—gentle it was as a bird's plumage—
And a shooting-

Star went by us on its errand elsewhere.
I knew neither astonishment nor fear
Till land glimmered below me, and an austere

Seaboard turf, shaggy as a wolf's pelt,
Bruised my being as I grounded with a jolt
On the prison-floor pavement

Of earth-bound man. The angels went smoothly on
Through a wilderness where each successive horizon
Was another sand dune.

Time held out no promise, for time was no more.
Bones and bleached tree roots lay scattered everywhere;
The dusk waited in vain for a star.

Suddenly the Cross scrambled off the bier.

Shouting like a bridegroom it bounded
On its one foot towards a pit dug in the sand—
A dark hole like a wound.

Poised on the edge of the pit, it began to sing.
"Lulla—lulla—lullaby" it sang. "I am home again."
And leaped in.

I saw the sand close over the pit and the suspended grey
Dusk convert to darkness in the twinkling of an eye.
"Now wake," said the angel, "and go your way."

THREE CONCRETE POEMS

WAYNE WESTLAKE

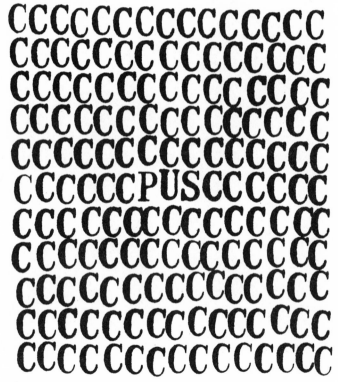

"Vitamin C Has Reduced the Pus"

W. Westlake '79

"PUPULE" BY WAYNE WESTLAKE

EGGS

EGGS

EGGS

EGGS

EGGS

EGGS

EGGS

EGGS

EGGS

EGGS

EGGS

EGGS

EGGS

EGGS

EGGS

EGGS

HMIO
AYSF
LFFF
FAA
  CL
  EL
  LI
    N
    G

BY WAYNE WESTLAKE

NOTES ON CONTRIBUTORS

BETSY ADAMS, who is working toward her Ph.D. in evolutionary ecology, has had two books of poetry published to date. "The Red Envelope" is part of her novel entitled *the dead birth, itself.*

Born in France in 1923, YVES BONNEFOY has published poetry, criticism, and translations in that country. *On the Motion and Immobility of Douve,* probably his best known work, is available from Ohio University Press in a translation by Galway Kinnell. SUSANNA LANG, who has also rendered into English Yves Bonnefoy's *Words in Stone* (University of Massachusetts, 1976), makes her home in Chicago.

After graduating from Stanford University, JANINE CANAN studied German literature at the University of California and was a teacher of language and literature for many years. She received her M.D. from New York University in 1976, completed her psychiatric residency at Mt. Zion Hospital in San Francisco, and is currently a practicing psychiatrist in Berkeley. Her first book of poems, *Of Your Seed,* was published by Oyez Press in 1977.

CAROL EMSHWILLER's collection of short stories, *Joy in Our Cause,* was published by Harper & Row, and she has completed a second collection tentatively entitled *Verging on the Pertinent.* Her work has appeared in several literary publications, including ND22.

Earlier this year, New Directions brought out a signed, limited edition of LAWRENCE FERLINGHETTI's book of poems *A Trip to Italy & France.* His *Endless Life: The Selected Poems,* which includes the "First Populist Manifesto," is due out in the spring.

RUSSELL HALEY lives in New Zealand, where his first collection of stories, *The Sauna Bath Mysteries,* was published in 1978. Earlier publications, of poetry, were *The Walled Garden* (1972) and *On the Fault Line* (1977). He is now working on an extended but discontinuous narrative called *Northern Lights*.

A native of Greensboro, North Carolina, WALTER HOWERTON worked as a reporter and editor for newspapers in the Carolinas, Georgia, and New Mexico for nine years. He completed work last year on his M.F.A. degree at the University of Iowa Writers Workshop, where he is now a doctoral candidate. His work has appeared in the *Carolina Quarterly*, and he is finishing his first novel.

For information on UCHIDA HYAKKEN, see the translator's introduction to "Kudan." NANCY BECKMAN pursued independent studies of traditional Japanese performing arts, language, and literature in Tokyo and Kyoto from 1971 to 1976. In 1978, she received her B.A. in East Asian Studies from Wesleyan University and since then has been preparing Japan-related cross-cultural materials for a student exchange program in co-operation with an educational project at Stanford University.

JAMES MCMANUS is the author of *Antonio Salazar Is Dead* (Syncline Press, 1979), a collection of twenty-six prose poems, six of which appear here. His work has appeared in *TriQuarterly*, the *Banyan Anthology, Kansas Quarterly*, and elsewhere. He currently holds an N.E.A. fellowship and is completing a novel.

Born in Buffalo, New York, in 1947, ANDREA MOORHEAD is the editor of *Osiris*, an international journal. Her work has appeared in *The Dalhousie Review, Prism International, L'Esprit Créateur, Sewanee Review*, and *Saint Andrews Review*.

MICHAEL MOTT's authorized biography of Thomas Merton is forthcoming from Houghton Mifflin. His poetry and prose have frequently appeared in such journals as *Encounter, Poetry, The Kenyon Review* (where he was poetry editor from 1967 to 1979) and in *The [London] Sunday Times*. He has published books of fiction and children's novels, and his new poetry collection, *Counting the Grasses*, was brought out in 1980 by Antigua Press. He is presently a Guggenheim Fellow.

JULIA OLDER is the recipient of a Hopwood Poetry Award from the University of Michigan and has been poet-in-residence at Yaddo, the MacDowell Colony, and the Ossabaw Foundation. She has completed a novel about New England Victorian poet Celia Thaxter and is now working on a book of poems and accompanying wood-cuts in her 6 x 8 foot New Hampshire studio. "A Paper Story" comes from *Oonts & Others*, a collection of narrative poems.

In 1979, New Directions brought out *A Draft of Shadows and Other Poems* by OCTAVIO PAZ in a bilingual edition. The British poet and critic CHARLES TOMLINSON has published several books of poetry with Oxford University Press, studies of Dante and of the sonnet with San Marcos and Folcroft, and a book of graphics with Persea.

JÁNOS PILINSZKY was born in 1921, and is generally regarded as Hungary's foremost avant-garde poet of the generation that became prominent after World War II. Two collections of his work are available in this country—*Crater: Poems 1974 to 1975* from Anvil Press and *Selected Poems* from Persea Books. EMERY GEORGE teaches German, comparative literature, and Hungarian poetry at the University of Michigan at Ann Arbor. He has published nine books, including four of poetry and two of translations from the Hungarian of Miklós Radnóti (Ardis, 1977 and 1980). He is at present editing an anthology of contemporary East European poetry.

Reminiscences of the late NORMAN HOLMES PEARSON (1909-1975) are contained in Aleksis Rannit's introduction to "Thirteen Draw-ings from the Norman Holmes Pearson Collection." Curator of Rus-sian and East European Studies at Yale, ALEKSIS RANNIT is one of the foremost poets in the Estonian language. A selection of his first assays in English appeared in ND41.

Born in 1945, WILL STAPLE has spent twenty Easters in the Grand Canyon and has lived for the last ten years mostly in waterless, one-board-thick shacks in the Northern California foothills. He is a carpenter, palm reader, and area coordinator for California Poets in the Schools and has published two books of poetry—*Passes for Hu-man* (Shaman Drum, 1978) and *Coyote Run* (with Anderson and Levant; Riverside, 1977).

GANGA PRASAD VIMAL was born forty years ago in Utrakashi, in the foothills of the Himalayas. He has studied at Allahabad and Punjab universities and presently teaches at Delhi University. His novels, short stories, poetry, and literary criticism in Hindi have earned him a place among the leading Indian writers of his generation. The late MILLEN BRAND's verse journal of his *Peace March*—at age seventy-one—from Nagasaki to Hiroshima with the Japanese peace marchers in 1977 was published last year by the Countryman Press. Brand was a poet and novelist. The poems included here were first rendered into the literal English from the Hindi by translator RATTAN CHOUHAN.

ISABELLA WAI holds an M.A. in Creative Writing and obtained her Ph.D. in English at McMaster University in Ontario. Her work has previously appeared in *Heavenly Bread* (Hong Kong), *Daedalian Quarterly* (Texas), *Brushfire* (Nevada), *Cumberlands* (Kentucky), *Wind Literary Journal* (Kentucky), and *Origins* (Ontario).

The late British author SYLVIA TOWNSEND WARNER (1893-1978) produced in her lifetime seven novels, seven volumes of short stories, four books of poetry, a collection of essays, and a biography of one of her staunchest admirers, T. H. White. "Twelve Poems" was read by Sir Peter Pears at the 1977 Adelburgh Festival and was broadcast after her death in 1978, and later published in the U.K. by Chatto & Windus.

The *Paris Review* Khan Prize for fiction was awarded to PAUL WEST in 1974. His most recent novel, *The Very Rich Hours of Count von Stauffenburg*, was brought out by Harper & Row in 1980.

WAYNE WESTLAKE was born in Lahaina, Maui, in Hawaii. His work has appeared locally in Honolulu, nationally across the Mainland, and internationally in Japan, Canada, Australia, and England.

Art critic, poet, fiction writer, and professor of English at Queens College of the City University of New York, HARRIET ZINNES is the editor of *Ezra Pound and the Visual Arts*, which New Directions published in 1980. Her latest collection of poetry, *Book of Ten*, will be brought out by Bellvue Press this year.